"How many women are you, Pepper?"
Thor asked seriously.

She looked at him, something unreadable flickering in her eyes. And then she was smiling, a smile as mysterious as his own. "As many as I have to be."

"That admission is a challenge to any man," Thor pointed out softly. "Like looking at a diamond with countless facets, or a puzzle with countless pieces. Something that has to be—must be—understood."

"Some puzzles can't be solved," Pepper said softly. "All I'm telling you, Thor, is, *be warned*. If you decide to study the diamond's facets or put the puzzle together, you may be biting off more than you can chew. Because while you're looking for solutions, I might very well decide that you're just what I've been looking for . . ."

WHAT ARE *LOVESWEPT* ROMANCES?

They are stories of true romance and touching emotion. We believe those two very important ingredients are constants in our highly sensual and very believable stories in the *LOVESWEPT* line. Our goal is to give you, the reader, stories of consistently high quality that may sometimes make you laugh, sometimes make you cry, but are always fresh and creative and contain many delightful surprises within their pages.

Most romance fans read an enormous number of books. Those they truly love, they keep. Others may be traded with friends and soon forgotten. We hope that each *LOVESWEPT* romance will be a treasure—a "keeper." We will always try to publish

*LOVE STORIES YOU'LL NEVER FORGET
BY AUTHORS YOU'LL ALWAYS REMEMBER*

The Editors

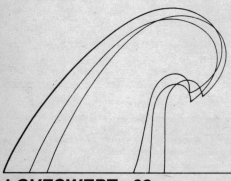

LOVESWEPT • 62

Kay Hooper
Pepper's Way

BANTAM BOOKS
TORONTO • NEW YORK • LONDON • SYDNEY • AUCKLAND

PEPPER'S WAY

A Bantam Book / September 1984

LOVESWEPT and the wave device are trademarks of Bantam Books, Inc.

ISBN 0-553-21668-6

Published simultaneously in the United States and Canada

Bantam Books are published by Bantam Books, Inc. Its trademark, consisting of the words ''Bantam Books'' and the portrayal of a rooster, is Registered in U.S. Patent and Trademark Office and in other countries. Marca Registrada. Bantam Books, Inc., 666 Fifth Avenue, New York, New York 10103.

PRINTED IN THE UNITED STATES OF AMERICA

O   0 9 8 7 6 5 4 3 2 1

One

WANTED: MAN. Must be over six feet tall and weigh at least two hundred pounds. Must own large house on considerable acreage. Must like animals. Must have job with flexible hours. Preferably single. Call Pepper.

He wouldn't have given the ad a second glance if he'd found it in the personals column of some trashy magazine. It certainly sounded typical of that kind of publication. And yet . . . Thor looked at the ad for the fifth time in as many minutes. Well, he fit all the requirements. And he was dying to find out what kind of woman would place such an ad in a large daily newspaper.

He'd seen the ad every day this week, and had grown more and more curious. And since he knew very well that the newspaper in which the ad was running didn't pander to lonelyhearts or practical jokers, he couldn't help but wonder exactly what it was all about. A publicity stunt or something. Had to be. But if it *wasn't* . . . well, then, what was it?

He possessed two overwhelming sins, neither of which was appropriate in his profession: curiosity and a love of the absurd. Sighing, he reached for the phone and dialed the number printed after the name Pepper.

"Hello?"

It was a sweet, childish voice, presently filled with suspicion. She sounded as though she might possibly be five years old . . . on her next birthday.

"Pepper?" he asked cautiously.

"Yes?" Definitely wary now.

"I'm calling about your ad," Thor began.

"Oh, Lord—another one! Listen, I'm pulling that ad tomorrow, so forget it! I've been listening to obscene suggestions all week, and I'm fed up! So, whoever you are, get your kicks somewhere else!"

The voice, he reflected, was still sweet and childish, but this was definitely no little girl he was talking to. Curiosity grew. Mildly, he told her, "I didn't call to make obscene suggestions."

"You didn't? Then what do you want?" she demanded.

"I thought it was a matter of what *you* wanted," he murmured. "A man over six feet tall, two hundred pounds—and so on."

"Do you fit?" she asked, still suspicious.

"Yes."

"How old are you?"

"Does that matter?"

She sighed, irritated. "I've had calls from four high school quarterbacks this week, and I didn't like any of their questions."

"High school is definitely behind me," he

responded, then asked in spite of himself, "What did they ask you?"

Clearly aggrieved, she said, "Well, one of them asked if I like leather. The other questions weren't repeatable."

Trying not to laugh, Thor said, "Your ad is a bit . . . suggestive."

"It is? But I spent so much time on the wording just to get the proper effect!" she wailed softly.

"The effect you got was far from proper. What, by the way, is the ad all about? You'll notice," he added virtuously, "that I'm not leaping to conclusions."

"I'll bet you leaped to plenty before you picked up the phone," she muttered, and then sighed again. "You see, it's my dog."

"Your dog?" Thor echoed.

"Uh-huh. My landlord found out. That is, he'd known that I *had* a dog, but he got all upset with me last week. Said something about not realizing that I fed it hay. Anyway, I can't keep my dog in this apartment anymore."

"I see." The matter was, indeed, becoming plainer to Thor. "Which is why you advertised for a large man with a house in the country."

"Right." She sounded relieved. "I mean, a small man would feel intimidated by a Dobe, don't you think?"

Thor, whose mind couldn't instantly identify *Dobe* to conjure a picture, agreed wholeheartedly. "Certainly. I suppose you'll want to know how large my house is?"

"You mean, you're interested?"

"Of course." Thor looked around at his large, spotless living room and heard his housekeeper banging pots in the kitchen. Ah, well. He could keep the dog outside; he needed a watchdog anyway. Pepper's voice intrigued him; he would have offered to look at a Bengal tiger if she'd asked. "Are you selling the dog, or—"

"Oh, no!" She was shocked. "I wouldn't do that!"

So she was just finding the dog a good home. Odd how some people felt better about giving away their pets rather than selling them. "I see. Well, Pepper—" He hesitated. "I'm sorry, but you didn't tell me your last—"

"Oh, everybody calls me Pepper," she assured him cheerfully. "Who are *you*, by the way?"

Thor found himself smiling. "Thorton Spicer. My friends call me Thor."

"I'll bet you have red hair."

Surprised, he confirmed her guess. "Yes, I do, but how did you know?"

"Vikings," she said cryptically, then went on as if no explanation were necessary. "Do you have a large house?"

"Four bedrooms, two baths, living room, den, study—"

"That sounds perfect! Land?"

"Fifteen acres." He was growing more and more amused. But he warned himself not to develop a mental picture of Pepper; whenever he did that, he was always disappointed. Of course, his mind was already busy drawing. Pepper, it decided arbitrarily, was about five feet tall with blond hair and big blue eyes. He told his mind not to be so damn sure. She was probably six feet tall with black hair and played hockey.

"Perfect!" The little breathless voice sounded delighted. "Oh, but, you'd better—"

"See the dog," he finished dryly. "Yes, perhaps

I'd better. I'm heading into town this afternoon; if you'll tell me where you live, I'll stop by."

She gave him clear, precise directions to her apartment building, which rather surprised him; she had sounded a bit feather-headed. Then she finished with, "You can't miss it"—which made him immediately distrust the directions. But he promised to drop by around three o'clock.

Before she could respond, there was a loud crash from her end, and she said hurriedly, "Oh, heavens! Brutus! What're you—? Look what you've done! Um, I'll see you at three."

Thor found himself listening to a dial tone, and assumed in amusement that the last sentence had been intended for him. He hung up the phone, chuckling quietly. Well, it would certainly be interesting meeting Pepper. And he *did* need a watch-dog. Brutus? He scaled his mental image of a Dobe up a few inches. Obviously a large dog. And why did the name keep ringing warning bells in his mind?

"Your lunch is getting cold," Mrs. Small told him dourly from the doorway of the room.

Mrs. Small wasn't. By any stretch of the imagination. She was only a little over five feet tall, but made up for the lack in other areas. All other areas. And she was the exception to the rule that all plump people were jolly souls. In five years Thor had never seen her so much as smile. He'd even given in to the lesser side of himself and tried a few practical jokes, only to be told coldly that he was too old for such nonsense.

Thor looked at her now and decided not to tell her about the possible addition to his household. "I told you not to bother," he said instead.

"No bother, as long as you eat it."

He wondered vaguely if Mrs. Small would ever call him by his name. Either of his names. She never had. He was almost terrified of the woman. "I'm coming," he said hastily, noting that her habitual frown was assuming thunderous proportions.

She deepened her glare, nodded briefly, and turned away.

Thor sighed and got to his feet. He headed for the dining room—Mrs. Small would *never* feed him in the kitchen!—wondering if Pepper would live up to his mind's optimism.

At exactly three o'clock Thor was standing before the door marked 3-B and silently bracing himself to be disappointed. He looked down at his neat dark slacks, white shirt, and sport jacket, and thought wryly that most people probably didn't care how they dressed to meet a dog. But then . . . he was meeting a woman. At least he hoped she was a woman.

He made a mental note to write to the friend from his college days, who now ran a rather lucrative dating service. If Jim hadn't tried inserting peculiar ads in newspapers, he was missing a good bet. . . .

Thor knocked on the door. A deep-throated "Woof!" and various other indefinable sounds came from within. Then the door swung open.

"Come in," a sweet, breathless voice invited. "If you're Thor, that is."

"I'm Thor," he managed, stepping inside automatically. The door closed behind him while he tried to collect himself. It wasn't easy; his mental picture of Pepper had been uncannily on target.

Since she was in socks only, he could gauge her height nicely; if she was stretched on a rack for ten minutes, she might possibly be five feet tall. Her hair was so light that *silver* was the only color that could describe it, and it fell nearly to her hips. Her face was finely drawn and delicate, and flattered the word *beautiful.* Only her eyes varied from his image, and he was glad they did; plain blue could never begin to compare with that glorious pale violet.

And—though tiny she certainly was—the mature and somewhat startlingly voluptuous curves filling out her jeans and knit top belonged only to a woman.

"I'm glad you found the place," she was telling him in that ridiculously intriguing little-girl voice. "Would you like to sit down, or—"

A loud thump from somewhere in one of the other rooms interrupted her, and she half turned from Thor, exclaiming fretfully, "Oh, damn, he got out!"

Before Thor could ask the foreboding question in his mind, a two-pound fury hurtled across the carpeted floor, uttering a hysterical yapping sound, and attached itself ferociously to his trouser leg. On closer inspection the fury turned out to be a Chihuahua that would have had to be dipped in milk and rolled in bread crumbs to weigh two pounds. It was light brown in color, and obviously possessed the temper and general disposition of a drunken marine.

In patient silence Thor shifted his weight onto his unencumbered leg and raised the other about a foot off the floor. The fury clung tenaciously, growling and trying fiercely to bring down its intended prey, entirely unperturbed by the fact that it was hanging in midair. Thor returned the foot and attached dog to the floor and lifted his eyes to Pepper. She was, he noted, looking down at the tiny dog with a fondly exasperated expression.

"What's it doing?" Thor asked politely.

Pepper looked up, surprised. "He's attacking you, obviously. He's an attack dog."

Thor looked hard for mockery on the lovely face, and found only solemnity. "Oh. Do you mind calling him off?"

"Well . . . I can't."

"You can't?" Thor decided that if both Pepper and this Lilliputian canine thought that it was an attack dog, who was he to argue? "I thought there was a command to call them off."

"There is," she agreed cheerfully. "It's 'break.' But Brutus ignores it; he always has."

Incredulously Thor dropped his gaze to the tiny creature. "*This* is Brutus? You can't tell me your landlord objects to this little mite!"

"Of course not. *Fifi*'s the problem."

"Fifi?" Thor decided that he had wandered through Alice's mirror by accident. The scary part was that he was enjoying it. "Uh . . . where's Fifi?"

Looking surprised again, Pepper half turned and gestured toward the couch a few feet away. Thor's gaze followed her pointing finger, and he immediately understood her surprise; his only excuse for having missed seeing the creature until now was that he'd been too fascinated by Pepper to look at his surroundings.

"Fifi" was a respectably sized mountain of short gleaming black and tan fur, quivering from pointed little ears to stub of a tail. It was lying on its belly with its face thrust underneath the couch, and a quick and rough calculation told Thor that it would be nearly three feet tall on all fours.

It was a full-grown and heavily muscled Doberman pinscher, which Thor had always considered one of the wickedest-looking dogs in creation. And it weighed every ounce of a hundred pounds.

The landlord's horror, he reflected, was now perfectly clear. He tried to picture the expression on Mrs. Small's face when she saw Fifi and hastily abandoned the effort when the first fleeting image came to his mind.

"Fifi?" Pepper called softly, and the dog quivered even more, not moving an inch.

"What's it doing?" Thor asked curiously.

"She's hiding."

"What's she hiding?"

"Herself."

"But I can see—"

"Shhh!" Pepper made a hasty gesture to silence him. "*She* thinks she's hiding. Since she can't see you, she thinks you can't see her."

Thor decided to let that pass; for the life of him, he didn't know how to respond. He realized suddenly that he was still being savaged. "Look, can you get this dog off my leg? I'm going to look a little peculiar walking around with him attached to me like this."

Pepper looked down at Brutus, frowned for a moment, then stepped closer. She bent over and swatted the tiny dog firmly on the rump. Immediately he whirled to contend with the surprise attack, and she snatched him up and tucked him under her arm. Apparently still blind with rage, Brutus was on the point of sinking his teeth into her arm when her voice stopped him cold.

"Don't . . . you . . . dare," she told him in an unexpectedly icy tone.

Pointed ears that were overlarge on the tiny head perked up, and there was such a ludicrously expressive "Oh, it's *you*!" look on the dog's face that Thor burst out laughing. Brutus immediately threw a snarl his way, clearly trying to save face.

"What do you feed him—gunpowder?"

"Of course not. I told you he was an attack dog." She waved a hospitable hand toward the small living room they were literally standing in. "Why don't you sit down? On the couch there, by Fifi. She'll come out once she gets used to your voice."

Thor went over to the couch, making a lengthy detour around Fifi's ample rump to sit a prudent distance away from her. He was taking no chances.

Pepper sat across from him in a chair, holding the ever-growling Brutus firmly in her lap. "Are you still interested?" she asked wryly.

Looking at her instead of the dog, Thor murmured, "More than ever."

If she heard anything in his voice to suggest that it was she, rather than her dog, that Thor was interested in, Pepper didn't show it on her face. She was completely natural, and obviously didn't possess a single coquettish bone in her body.

And she didn't, Thor reflected thankfully, weigh him with a speculative and unnerving eye, as so many women seemed to do these days. He wondered suddenly if she were as old as her body suggested.

"How old are you?" he demanded abruptly.

Pepper seemed neither surprised nor offended by the question. Instead, she released a long-suffering sigh. "*Et tu, Brute*? I'm twenty-eight." At his obvious surprise she added dryly, "I have to carry a special police identification card because nobody ever believes that. Shall I show it to you?"

Thor grinned. "No need; I'll take your word for it."

"Thanks. And you never told me how old you are, by the way."

"Thirty-four. And nobody *ever* disbelieves that."

She studied him with a total lack of self-consciousness. "I can see how they wouldn't," she said ingenuously. "You have a rough sort of face; it has a history."

Thor immediately felt at least ten years older than he was. History? Glancing aside to collect his thoughts, he found himself under scrutiny from a pair of panicky brown eyes that widened in even greater panic and then disappeared. Fifi was hiding again. Thor looked at Pepper, and she shrugged, giving him a rueful smile.

"She'll get used to you."

"She's a coward," he observed dryly.

"Well . . . I guess you could say that. She barks once and then hides."

Thor remembered the deep-throated bark he'd heard. "Uh-huh. Some watchdog she's going to make."

Pepper smiled at him happily, the bottomless pools of her violet eyes oddly riveting. "Are you saying that you want her?"

He didn't even hesitate. "Definitely. But I don't know about taking her with me today. She's so nervous, and my car—"

"What kind of car do you have?"

"A Corvette."

Pepper winced. "That'll never do. Tell you what. I have a van, so why don't I do the relocating? We can come tomorrow."

Convinced that Pepper wouldn't abandon her pet totally, Thor nodded and smiled. "Sounds great. You can help her with the—uh—transitional period."

"Wonderful! What time tomorrow shall we come?"

"Any time after noon."

"We'll be there." Pepper looked down at the huge, quivering dog, and smiled fondly. "I'm sure she'll be braver in the country."

Thor blinked and then looked down at the dog as well. He'd nearly forgotten about Fifi. "Uh . . . yes. I'm sure she will be."

Two

Gray eyes, Pepper thought, leaning back against the closed door and staring absently across the room. He had gray eyes. Combined with his red-gold hair and deeply tanned skin, the gray eyes were startling. They were also sharp, intelligent, and held a lurking twinkle.

Releasing her pent-up breath in a long sigh, Pepper bent to set Brutus on the floor. She saw that her hands were shaking and wasn't surprised by that. But she was surprised by her reaction to Thor Spicer. At twenty-eight she'd ruefully decided that she would probably remain unattached, because she had not, in all her travels, met a man whose voice set her heart bumping and raised goose bumps on her flesh.

Almost reluctantly she lifted an arm and examined her lightly tanned skin. Uh-huh. Gooseflesh.

And heaven knew her heart was bumping against her ribs as though she'd been running.

Still leaning against the door, she watched Fifi rise, shake herself, then wag a happy bobtailed rear end and follow Brutus toward the kitchen and their food dishes. Pepper shook her head slightly. What had her *brilliant* newspaper ad gotten her into? Simply because she'd wanted to find Fifi a good home with a kind man . . .

The truth floated into her consciousness gently, unthreateningly: like most of the schemes and plans her active mind spawned, this idea had looked innocent and logical on the surface. Experience had taught her that her "logical" plans generally possessed hidden pitfalls. However, she'd never given up her scheming just because of a few minor stumbling blocks.

Cal's voice surfaced suddenly in her mind, a little desperate and a lot wild: "You're dangerous, you know that? You're *ruthless* and, God, who'd guess it by looking at you?"

Pepper grinned to herself. That had been wailed at her just moments before Cal's wedding to Marsha five years ago, and just after a long and somewhat involved courtship in which Pepper had played a vital role. Matchmaker. She was good at that.

After all, Cal and Marsha were still married, and very happily so from the looks of it. And the other matches she'd engineered over the years were still going strong, not a divorce or separation in the lot.

This time Johnny's voice popped into her mind: "Let's all band together and get Pepper settled; it'd be poetic justice! She's the only one of the gang still footloose and fancy-free."

Absently Pepper moved over to sink down on the

couch, drawing her legs up and tucking her feet under a cushion. The gang was indeed all settled. Most within driving distance of one another in the Northeast; she, herself, was the farthest north at the moment, living in Maine. Her original college crowd numbered nearly a score—and that wasn't counting the strays she'd happened across on her travels and brought home to be matched with her friends.

Ruthless? She thought about that for a moment. Certainly she was ruthless. But she would never do anything to hurt a friend—which was probably why she had so many of them. She was also a helluva lot smarter than she looked, and perfectly capable of taking care of herself even in the turmoil of Third World countries.

So, being a smart and ruthless lady, she had never yet hesitated to go after what she wanted, be it a seat on a booked airline or some trinket requiring haggling in a language she didn't speak.

But a man? No, she'd never gone after a man. Heaven knew she had plenty of male friends spread out over the world. But no gooseflesh. Until now.

She grinned to herself. "Okay, Pepper," she murmured out loud, "how do you propose to do the thing? And never mind the idea. The idea is dumb . . . and dangerous." She brooded silently for a moment.

"He's interested. That was obvious. I don't know why, but he is." She winced as Fifi clambered up onto her lap—all hundred pounds of her. Stroking the sleek fur, Pepper gazed sternly into mild brown eyes. "He didn't want you, old girl. I'm sure he'll give you a good home, and love you once he gets to know you. But curiosity brought him here. He wasn't interested in a hundred-pound lap dog.

However . . . he *said* he wants you. I wonder if he realizes I won't totally abandon you to a stranger?"

Fifi whined what could have been taken for an agreement.

"I wonder exactly how far his interest goes?" Pepper mused to her sympathetic canine friend. "He doesn't look like the home-and-hearth type. I was right; his face has a history. That little scar above his left eye . . . And he looks tired. I wonder what he does for a living? Something out in the weather. That's not a swimming-pool tan, and his hands have seen rough use. And he's strong."

Fifi saluted her mistress's cheek with a tongue the size of a hand towel and smiled all over her face.

"Thank you," Pepper told the dog dryly. "I'll certainly try to justify your faith in me." She managed to worm her way out from under Fifi, knowing from experience that it was much easier to move herself than to move the huge dog. Absently she paced over to the sliding glass doors that opened onto her balcony. Then, turning away a moment later, she caught her reflection in an ornate mirror on the wall and paused to study herself critically.

"If only you were a few inches taller," she told the frowning reflection mournfully. "And brunet. And busty." She turned sideways and stuck out her chest experimentally. The experiment wasn't a complete success; she looked decidedly off-balance and rather ridiculous.

Sighing, Pepper turned away from the reflection and assumed her normal posture. "Face it," she told herself aloud in a firm voice. "You'll just have to do the best you can with the material available."

She paced restlessly around the room, only vaguely noticing that Brutus had returned from the kitchen and taken up a heel position, pacing along beside her like a diminutive sentry. She thought back over the years, reviewing the personalities and appearances of various men who'd crossed her path and expressed a preference for pint-size blondes.

Pepper had received more than one proposal during the past ten years and quite a few propositions, none of which she'd felt even mildly tempted to accept. For the most part, she reflected, men tended to treat her like a kid sister, but the ones who had felt romantically inclined had certainly tried hard enough to arouse the same reaction in her.

Self-confident without being at all vain, Pepper was always surprised by interest from a man; it was never something she expected. Generally content with her own appearance, she nonetheless fell prey to wishful thinking whenever confronted by a tall, graceful brunet woman. She was ruefully aware that it was impossible to be either graceful or striking when one was possessed of a snub nose and less than five feet of height.

The desire to change both characteristics had never been more than wistful . . . until just a few minutes ago . . . when she had opened the door to admit Thor Spicer. At that moment she had wanted desperately to grow six inches and acquire a thin, aristocratic nose.

The shrill demand of the phone yanked Pepper from her thoughts just then, and she went over to an end table to life the receiver.

"Hello? Oh, hello, Mr. Jacobs. Well . . . yes, I still have the dog, but— Yes, I know when I sublet the apartment I agreed— Yes, but— Mr. Jacobs, if you'll just let me tell you— I *know* how long it's been— Look, I'm trying to tell you—"

She felt an unaccustomed anger growing inside of her as she listened to the annoyed and repetitive voice of the building manager. And the idea she had firmly discarded, she realized later, began prodding her subconsciously . . . or at least that's how she excused herself forever afterward.

"Mr. Jacobs. Mr. Jacobs! Enough with the threats, all right? Nobody's complained to me about the dog except you, and I think— What? There's no need to be abusive! Fine. Fine. But you'd damn well better not rent this apartment to anyone else, because Miss James has a lease and it's paid up for months! And another thing: You're responsible for her furniture until she returns from Europe. I'll call her attorney tomorrow, and he'll be over to inventory every stick of furniture and every ornament in the place. And every bit of it had better *be* here when she gets home! Good-bye!"

Pepper slammed down the telephone and spent a few moments breathing quickly and feeling mildly surprised at her own anger. By nature she was a peacemaker and not given to outbursts—least of all with someone who had every right to be angry at her. She sat down on a chair and looked thoughtfully at her waiting canine audience.

"I believe I just burned my bridges," she told them slowly. "With a vengeance. My friends, we're about to embark on an all-out frontal assault. We're going to storm the battlements . . . march on the citadel . . . with banners flying and cannons at the ready." She giggled suddenly, nervously, at her own imagery, then sobered.

"I only hope that laugh I saw in his eyes was for

real. Otherwise he's going to repel this invasion with the greatest of ease!"

Thor found himself going to the front window for the tenth time in as many minutes, and swore softly. But he didn't leave the window. He stood looking out over his neatly manicured front lawn and thinking absently about the hours spent raking leaves over the past week. A calming pastime, and one he enjoyed whenever he was home. He'd be home now for several weeks. Time enough, he thought, to get to know a tiny blonde with the most incredible violet eyes he'd ever seen.

A motion on the edge of his line of sight caught his eye, and he turned his head to see Lucifer's sleek black head lift above the split-rail fence bordering the yard. The stark white diamond in the center of the stallion's forehead pointed toward the house, and he seemed to be watching intently. Thor pulled one hand from the pocket of his jeans and swept the drapes aside, giving the horse an indication of his presence.

Immediately Lucifer shied violently away from fence and house, a movement prompted by spirit rather than fear. He patrolled the fence for a few moments, head high, nostrils flaring, and long black tail held like a banner of pride, looking toward the window as if in invitation. Then he took off in a burst of speed, galloping toward his open stable in the little hollow below the house.

Thor felt a sudden uneasiness. Other than himself, Lucifer hated every living thing, and dogs topped his list of enemies. How he would react to "one of the hated" living with his master, Thor didn't even want to guess. He comforted himself with the reminder of Fifi's cowardice; she probably wouldn't go near the pasture, he decided. He hoped.

He started to turn away from the window when a motion from the opposite direction caught his attention. And as soon as his eyes focused on the predominantly white object, he realized that Pepper had arrived to effect the relocation of her pet.

She'd said she had a van, he remembered, but . . . "Good Lord," he murmured to himself, fascinated. Anyone, he decided, who could call that vehicle a van was prone to vast understatement. He made an absent mental note to remember Pepper's penchant in that regard and then stared at her vehicle again.

In the first place, it was not a van at all, but what was commonly called an RV—a recreational vehicle. And it was thirty-five feet long. Custom built from the looks of it, it boasted tinted windows along the sides; cheery bumper stickers and more prosaic state travel stickers were plastered everywhere; a blue and white awning was rolled up and tied in place above the door; and the whole was liberally splashed with mud.

Wondering how a woman as tiny as Pepper could wheel that monster into his driveway so neatly, Thor left the window and headed for his front door. And if he'd been fascinated yesterday, he was even more so now. From childhood he'd been drawn to the offbeat, the unusual—and it had led him into trouble more than once. It could, he knew, be leading him into trouble now. But the realization didn't cause him to falter.

He enjoyed trouble. Usually.

Shutting the front door behind him, Thor left the house and went down the walk to the paved driveway. He enjoyed the ludicrous contrast of his sleek Corvette and the hulking monster Pepper had parked behind it. The side door of the RV opened just as he reached it. Brutus leaped out first, lifting a lip at Thor but not wasting time with an attack because of his obvious desire to explore new surroundings.

Pepper got out of the vehicle in a no less sedate manner, jumping down without bothering to use the built-in step. Thor almost sighed aloud at the lovely picture she made in her neat jeans and pale blue sweater, her long hair caught up in a casual ponytail. And he forwent polite greetings out of the necessity to give a hasty warning.

"Better not let Brutus go near the pasture. If he attacks Lucifer, he'll learn how to 'break' the hard way."

"Lucifer?" she questioned over her shoulder, somewhat occupied with half lying inside the door of the RV and hanging onto the collar of a reluctant Fifi.

"My horse," he murmured, watching the struggle with interest and silently betting with himself on the outcome.

He lost the bet. Pepper emerged victorious from the struggle, hauling the hundred-pound dog out of the vehicle. Fifi immediately hid her face behind the woman, quivering.

"Is the name descriptive?" she asked, one delicate eyebrow rising.

" 'Fraid so."

Pepper looked around quickly and spotted the tiny dog near the rear of the RV. "Brutus, heel!" she ordered in that disconcertingly icy voice of command, and the voice was heeded as Brutus came to sit by her ankle.

"I thought he didn't obey," Thor noted in surprise.

"He obeys everything but 'break,' " Pepper told him cheerfully. "And I think he only ignores that because he likes attacking." Before he could respond, she was speaking once again in that little-girl, breathless voice that utterly fascinated Thor.

"Just look at the trees! They go on practically forever. You know, after I lived in a desert for six months, I learned to absolutely *adore* trees. I guess you can never know how much you will miss something until it isn't there."

"I guess." Thor watched her reach back to shut the door of the RV, feeling his mind drift gently into that bemused sphere that Pepper seemed to carry around with her. "You lived in a desert?"

"For a while. Never really liked it though. No trees. And I hate camels. What a beautiful house! I love the bay window. And that rock chimney! Is the fireplace rock?"

Trying not to laugh, Thor followed Pepper as she began to explore the outside of the house and the yard. "It's rock," he barely had time to answer, and then she was off again.

"Is that the barn down there in the hollow? Of course. What a beautiful horse! He looks so proud. Do you ever show him? Oh, I love your patio! What do you cook in that barbecue—a whole steer? Heel, Fifi, and stop being so silly; no one's going to hurt you! Out of the shrubs, Brutus, and heel, blast you!"

Having given up on his intention not to laugh, Thor just enjoyed the stroll around the house. He listened to Pepper's questions but didn't again try to answer them, content just to watch her profile and hear the lovely sound of her voice. And he wondered to himself if it would be possible to get to know this woman in a few short weeks.

And then her words penetrated, and he felt slightly bewildered for a moment to hear her voice his thoughts.

". . . and it'll only be for a few weeks, after all."

They had completely circled the house by then, coming to a halt back where they'd started beside the vehicles. Thor blinked and tried to concentrate. "I'm sorry. You were saying . . . ?"

"That it'll only be for a few weeks, three months at the most," she responded cheerfully. "When Kristen comes home, I'll be on my way again, so it's just until then. That English breeder carried her off with him just for the season, he *said.* Anyway, I think that paved area beside the garage will be perfect for the van. But we never discussed rent. I'll be quite happy to pay what the apartment was costing, if that sounds reasonable to you."

"Rent?" Thor managed blankly, wondering with an unfamiliar sense of desperation when he'd lost the thread of the conversation.

She looked surprised. "Of course! I mean, I wouldn't think of parking the van on your property and living here for weeks without paying rent. I'll need bathroom privileges too. I can hook up to that outside receptacle for power, but it's really not practical to hook up the water or septic tank for such a short time, don't you think?"

With her inquiring violent eyes on his face, Thor could only answer in one way. "Uh . . . of course. It's not practical at all."

Pepper nodded. "That's what I thought. Here, let me go ahead and park the van in place, so it'll be out of your way. Stay!" she ordered the two dogs firmly, casually guiding Thor's hand to grasp Fifi's collar. And then she opened the RV's door and climbed inside.

Thor found himself leaning back against the hood of the Corvette, holding a quivering Doberman by the collar and staring down at an obviously hostile and watchful Chihuahua. He lifted his gaze to watch Pepper, looking absurdly childlike through the driver's window, maneuver the RV expertly into place beside the garage without once getting into the grass or near his car.

Bemused, bewildered, and ruefully convinced that he'd wandered back through Alice's mirror, Thor was conscious of only one thought: It couldn't be this easy!

It can't be this easy, Pepper thought a little wildly, parking her van neatly beside the garage. She felt a giggle rise in her throat and let it emerge. Oh, his face! The poor man; she really should be ashamed of herself for barreling over him like a steamroller!

He'd taken it well, though, she thought in amusement. A blank look and then a blink—and then she'd seen that really marvelous gleam of laughter rise in his eyes.

And she didn't regret a thing. In fact, she'd never before been so glad that she'd followed her instincts and jumped headfirst into a situation without a lot of planning. Of course, it was quite possible that nothing would ever come of it.

Pepper felt something in that moment that she'd never felt before. A surge of emotion blocked her throat, and she hesitated for a minute before leaving the van.

What if nothing came of it?

A gambler at heart, and quite prepared to pay

whatever price was demanded for the chances she took, Pepper was fully and completely conscious for the first time of just what she was doing. She had never gambled for such high stakes, or bet so heavily on herself.

The game—for now, at least—was blindman's buff. Each bit of knowledge and understanding she could gain of him would light a dim candle, and with those candles she would have to find her way. The more she learned, the brighter the light to see by . . . to see if what she'd instantly felt for him was real . . . and to see if he could learn to feel the same for her.

Pepper squared her shoulders and reached for the door. Well, she had played more dangerous games—more dangerous to life and limb, that is. Not more dangerous to the heart. Danger didn't bother her. If one risked nothing, one gained nothing, after all.

So she was risking everything, her whole self, on one throw of the dice. And if what she felt was real, she meant to chase Thor as long and as far as it took. Until he caught her.

Emerging from the van and crossing over to where Thor and the pets waited, Pepper choked back a laugh at his still-bemused expression. She quickly began to speak. "You know, it's a good thing you answered my ad yesterday. My landlord called right after you left and threw me out. Wasn't that mean of him? He was supposed to give me more time."

Thor roused himself from some inner specula-tion. "I meant to ask why you lived in an apartment at all. Since you have the RV, I mean. Or isn't it yours?"

"Oh, it's mine." Pepper bent to pick up Brutus,

tucking him under an arm. "The apartment wasn't though. Not really. I sublet it from Kristen, primarily so that I could take care of her furniture and things while she was in England."

"A friend?" he guessed, feeling his way.

"A good friend. We met at Madison Square Garden in New York a couple of years ago at a dog show."

Thor glanced down at Fifi, who was sitting beside him and looking less nervous than he'd yet seen her. Then he looked at Brutus. "Which one were you showing?"

"Oh, neither. I was handling another friend's Great Dane. Kristen was handling a Dane, too, for a client of hers. We got our leashes tangled on the way to the ring, and one thing led to another. We've been friends ever since."

Thor nodded as if the meeting made perfect sense to him. "I see. Uh . . . why don't we go inside the house? I n— that is, I'd like to have a drink."

He thought that he saw a quick gleam of laughter in her eyes, but it was gone too rapidly for him to be sure. She looked anxiously from one dog to the other, then back up at his face.

"The dogs are very well mannered, but—"

"They're invited too." Thor sighed and started up the walk, automatically retaining his hold on Fifi's collar. "My housekeeper is off today, so she can't object."

"You have a housekeeper?" Pepper was walking beside him. "What's she like?"

Thor didn't answer until he'd opened the front door and stood aside for her to precede him. "Difficult," he pronounced finally.

Pepper halted in the doorway to give him a mischievous smile. "Ah. Your home is her castle?"

"Something like that." He followed her into the entranceway and shut the door behind them before releasing Fifi. A bit uneasy, he watched Pepper set Brutus down on the carpeted floor. "If he attacks me again . . ."

She looked back at him in surprise. "Of course, he won't. This is your house, not his. He may be a bit protective around the van once he realizes that we're staying here, but he won't attack you inside your own house."

Thor watched the little dog guardedly for a moment, then realized that Pepper knew what she was talking about. Brutus showed no disposition to savage his host, but set about immediately getting acquainted with the house.

"Let's have that drink first," Thor murmured finally. "Afterward I'll show you around the house if you like."

"I like." She smiled and then obeyed his slight gesture, preceding him and stepping down into the sunken den. Looking around the neat room, Pepper sighed with pleasure. It was decorated in shades of brown and rust and contained the comfortable overstuffed furnishings appropriate for a big man. "I don't know about the rest of the house, but this room is terrific."

"Glad you like it." Thor moved toward an unobtrusive bar in the corner by the bay window and sent a questioning glance toward her. "What's your poison?" he asked, his mind only half on the query as he realized how right she looked in his home. It was a very disconcerting observation.

"Oh, whatever you're having."

He paused for a moment. "I'm having whiskey. Straight."

"Fine." She laughed at his expression. "Thor, I'm

old enough to drink, you know. In fact, those who know me best claim that I have a cast-iron stomach." Wandering over to stand before the lovely rock fireplace, Pepper continued to smile at him. He seemed to be concentrating on fixing the drinks, and his next abrupt question nearly caught her off guard.

"Why did you advertise for a 'preferably single' man?"

Pepper waited to answer until he looked at her and appreciated the wry expression on her face. "Well, I hardly think a wife would welcome my camping out on her doorstep, do you? Of course . . . there's always the possibility of a girlfriend or fiancée objecting." It was a question, and Pepper didn't bother making any bones about it. The stakes were too high.

Thor picked up their glasses and carried hers across to her. When he handed her the glass, he shook his head slightly, and there was a tiny smile in his eyes. "Not in this case. My job takes me away from home too often to encourage . . . long-term relationships."

Pepper was quick to hear the note of constraint in his deep voice, so she passed on asking the next logical question. So he was touchy about his job, eh? Well, she could find out about that later. She raised her glass in a slight toast. "Then there's no problem."

His glass clinked softly against hers. "No problem at all."

She knew very well that he realized she hadn't initially planned on moving herself as well as the dog out here, and hoped that her mention of the landlord's having thrown her out would cover that. However, the whole situation was still full of holes, and her biggest hope was that Thor simply wouldn't question it.

Feeling suddenly breathless under the gaze of steady gray eyes, Pepper turned away and went over to sit down on the comfortable couch. The phone on the end table beside her set up a train of thought, and she looked across at Thor. "By the way, do you mind if I let my friends know where they can reach me by phone?"

"Of course not."

She grinned. "It's only fair to warn you. They're a talkative bunch. I'm liable to get calls pretty regularly. I'd hate to tie up your line."

Leaning against the mantel and watching her with a faint smile, Thor shrugged. "That's okay. I have another line in my bedroom for . . . important calls."

Again Pepper let the subject pass without a question, although she nearly had to bite her tongue to do it. "Great. Oh—we never settled on the rent."

"There's no hurry." Glancing toward the doorway, he found himself under scrutiny from Fifi's ridiculously worried brown eyes, and had to chuckle. "Unlike your former landlord, I won't kick you off the place."

"Whatever you say." Pepper sat back and sipped her drink slowly, wondering how to say what had to be said. She hesitated to assume an interest that had not yet been put into words, but she would have been less of a woman than she was to misinterpret the look in Thor's gray eyes.

His seemingly offhand remark about his work had told her two things, and she was sure that one meaning, at least, had been deliberately sent her way. He probably hadn't realized that she'd picked up some undercurrent concerning his job. Definitely, though, he had meant her to understand that long-term relationships weren't a part of his plans.

That didn't daunt Pepper; either he would change his mind or he wouldn't. And this man, she knew intuitively, would neither be pushed or led down the aisle. He would take that trip of his own free will, or he simply wouldn't go. And she wouldn't have had it any other way.

"You're very beautiful," he said suddenly, and immediately looked surprised, as if he hadn't intended to say those words aloud.

Pepper felt her heart give a bump, and sternly tried to control it. He had given her the opening she needed, and she had to take advantage of it. She looked down at the drink in her hand, then steadily back at him.

"I'm not very comfortable with oblique comments, Thor. I'm not very good at tiptoeing verbally around a subject. And since this situation is a bit out of the ordinary, well . . . I'll be blunt." She felt herself smiling wryly. "My friends say I'm good at that."

"Not interested, huh?" he asked lightly, but Pepper could feel his sudden tension. She didn't answer the question directly.

"I have rules, Thor."

"Rules?"

She looked at him steadily, and the honesty in her eyes told him that she was serious, that she meant whatever she was about to say.

"Rules. They're my rules, and they have nothing to do with morality. It's only that I know what would or wouldn't work for myself. And an affair wouldn't work for me."

"I see. Commitment."

Pepper dropped her gaze to the glass in her hand, and when she went on, her voice was quiet, musing. "There have been occasions during the last ten years when the opportunity was there. But something inside of me always said that what was right for the moment wouldn't be right for long. And I don't like regrets. Life's too short for regrets."

Watching her, Thor felt suddenly that there was a very definite reason for her last almost inaudible sentence. Her eyes were hidden from him, but her face was very still, and her voice seemed to have come from a great distance. She had some reason to avoid regrets, he thought, and wondered what it was.

She looked up suddenly, the violet eyes blurred for a moment. Then they were clear, and she was speaking in the same quiet, thoughtful voice as before.

"Commitment . . . yes. Something that's right for more than just the moment. Usually when people talk about a commitment between a man and woman, they mean marriage. Well, marriage seems to be entered into very lightly these days by a lot of people. But I don't happen to believe marriage is something you decide on with the idea in the back of your mind that it's a contract easily and amicably dissolved in court if it doesn't work. When I say 'till death do us part,' I expect to mean just that.

"And I *am* looking for that kind of permanence, Thor. I don't know if I'll find it—how can I know that? But one thing I do know: If I climb into a man's bed, or he climbs into mine, it has to be with the knowledge that I think I've found what I'm looking for. And he has to feel the same way."

She laughed suddenly and shortly in wry amusement. "And if that puts me in the company of dodos and dinosaurs"—she lifted her glass in a slightly mocking toast—"then here's to things past . . . but not forgotten."

After a moment Thor lifted his glass in an answering toast. In doing so, he was silently complimenting her honesty. But, more than that, he was admiring clear-sighted knowledge. She knew what she wanted, and she was unwilling to settle for less. And how many people, he wondered, were that lucky? How many people were spared blind searching because they had the foresight, the certain knowledge, of what they were searching for?

He watched her sip her drink, remembering suddenly the stillness of her face and the remark about no regrets. That expression had been oddly in contrast to his first impression of her. But, then, he had been constantly revising his first impression with every moment spent in her company. And the question that escaped him now was a little rueful, and more than a little bemused.

"How many women are you, Pepper?"

She looked at him, something unreadable flickering in her eyes. And then she was smiling, her smile as twisted and rueful as his own. "As many as I have to be." She finished her drink and set the glass down on the end table beside the phone.

"That admission is a challenge to any man," he pointed out softly. "Like looking at a diamond with countless facets, or a puzzle with countless pieces. Something that has to be—must be—understood."

"Some puzzles can't be solved because they're interpreted different ways by different people." Pepper looked intently at him, determined in her innate honesty that he wouldn't think her rules were easily overcome. "Like the Lady and the Tiger. If you were that man, Thor, and you opened the door your princess had told you to open, what do you think you would find?"

Thor looked at her searchingly, aware that she was telling him something. And he felt that what she was trying to tell him was important. Slowly he said, "I think if I opened the door she told me to open, I'd find the lady behind it."

Pepper rose to her feet, sliding her hands into the pockets of her jeans and shaking her head slightly. "And I think you'd find the Tiger. Princesses—women—were ruthless in those days, Thor. We still are. Abstract reasoning doesn't appeal to us much. We decide things by feelings more often than not. Our own feelings."

"What are you telling me?" he asked bluntly. "That your rules are yours, and therefore inviolable?"

Peeper laughed suddenly. Only a few candles had been lit, but already she saw her way clearly. And, true to her nature, she stepped forward boldly to begin the journey.

"What I'm telling you, Thor, is—*be warned.* If you decide to study the diamond's facets, or put the puzzle together, you may be biting off more than you can chew. Lord, we're mixing metaphors right and left. Because while you're looking for solutions, I might very well decide that you're just what I've been looking for."

Thor was slowly beginning to smile. "And so?"

"And, so, I'm a ruthless woman. I hate to lose." Pepper smiled at him very sweetly. "I'd chase you to hell and back, O god of thunder. And not even Odin—or your magic hammer—could save you."

Three

Thor's laugh began as a rumble deep inside his chest, growing slowly into the delighted sound of pure enjoyment. She'd flung the gauntlet at his feet, the little witch! She'd neatly picked up his earlier hint of no long-term involvement, flatly laid down her own rules, and then gently dared him to match wits with her. Challenged him . . . and he'd never had a more intriguing challenge.

Still chuckling, he put his empty glass down on the mantel and moved slowly toward her with the unthinking grace of a cat. "You realize, of course," he told her conversationally, "that I can't possibly ignore your challenge."

"The thought did occur," she murmured, watching his approach and still smiling. Not quite as calm as she appeared, Pepper was tautly aware that this would be the moment of truth. In the next few minutes one of two things would happen.

Either she would know that she'd been wrong about her feelings for this almost stranger—in which case she would fold her tent and steal quietly away—or she would discover that the feelings would indeed be there. And there would be no turning back.

"I've always loved challenges. I would have wanted to open Pandora's box," he said, halting less than an arm's length away and looking down at her with lazily smiling eyes.

"Never know what might jump out at you," she warned softly, tilting her head back to look up at him.

Thor reached out slowly, one large hand nearly encircling her neck, his thumb brushing along her jawline. "I think," he murmured as his head bent toward hers, "I'll take my chances."

Pepper didn't know what she had expected. A pleasant tingle, perhaps. A firecracker or two. She'd even wondered if Marsha had been right with her "Bells, my dear—ringing their little clangers off." But, being realistic, she had expected nothing so drastic. Just a sign, a preview of marvelous things to come.

What she got was the main attraction, and she very nearly forgot who had challenged whom.

For a still, timeless moment his lips rested on hers with the weight of a feather and the force of a sigh. Warm, undemanding, faintly questioning—and she was astonished at her response. The shivering tingle began somewhere near her middle, sweeping outward in ripples of curiously hot-cold sensation. She was only dimly aware of her hands leaving the pockets of her jeans and sliding up around his neck, helpless to prevent her lips from parting and inviting his exploration.

And the hot-cold sensation blazed suddenly white-hot, sizzling through her veins and scorching nerve endings as he abruptly accepted her invitation. His lips slanted across hers with driving hunger, demanding, compelling, sapping the strength from her legs.

Pepper was conscious of an aching emptiness within her, a throbbing hollowness she had never felt before. It seemed to fill her being, hot and hurting with an unfamiliar pain. She felt driven to be closer to him, hungry to touch him and have him touch her.

The sensations frightened her in their intensity; they swept aside logic and rationality to leave only raw emotion. But what frightened her even more was that the raw emotion was stronger than fear, stronger than her ability to fight it. She couldn't break away from him even with her instincts for self-preservation clamoring a desperate warning.

Those instincts told her that she'd met her match this time, that the stakes were higher than she had known. Her challenge had left her vulnerable to an intensity of feeling she'd not been prepared for, and she wondered dimly what price would be demanded of her this time for the reckless chance she had taken.

Then the fire in her veins blazed over fear, and she was conscious only of her need for this man. She had no strength left, no power over her own body. She was weightless and adrift on a churning sea, and there was no life preserver to save her from drowning. . . .

Thor's lips left hers as she was going down for the second time, and he drew a deep breath as if he, too, had nearly drowned.

Pepper stared dazedly into storm-clouded gray

eyes and, incurably honest, said exactly what she was thinking. "Pandora's box. I think we're both in trouble."

"I think you're right," Thor said a bit raggedly. "Good Lord, for such a little thing, you pack one hell of a punch, lady."

"You know what they say about dynamite." She wondered idly how she could possibly be having a perfectly rational conversation while looking eye-to-eye with a man who'd just demonstrated the Fourth of July in the middle of October. . . . Eye-to-eye? That wasn't right!

Leaning a bit sideways, Pepper looked down and realized only then why she felt so weightless: she was being held a good foot off the floor for Pete's sake. Returning her gaze to Thor's still-bemused face, she requested politely, "Could you put me down, please?"

"No," he said simply.

Pepper stared at him. "Why not?"

Thor kissed her very lightly. Then he kissed her lightly again, wearing the pleased expression of a man who has discovered a wonderful new hobby. "Because, like Brutus," he murmured, "I ignore the command to 'break.' "

She bit her lip to hold back an ill-timed giggle. "I did say please."

"I can't seem to hear that either. Although, if it were stuck in the right sentence—"

"Forget it, chum." She unlocked one hand from his hair and waved a threatening finger beneath his nose. "Remember the Alamo!"

He lifted an eyebrow. "No quarter?"

"No quarter. No mercy. One of us is going to break. And, as the man said, it ain't gonna be me."

"Want to bet?"

"We already did."

"True."

"Are you going to put me down?"

"No."

"You're vulnerable, you know. There are pressure points in your neck. And, of course, I could always resort to the old both-hands-clapped-to-the-ears trick. It shatters the eardrums, I'm told."

Thor looked at her consideringly. "You've learned to take care of yourself."

"Yes." She didn't elaborate.

"I get the feeling you've had an interesting life."

"Perhaps. But, interesting or not, I have no intention of discussing my past while dangling in the air."

"Will you discuss it if I put you down?"

"Maybe."

"Uh-uh." Thor shook his head. "If I've learned anything at all about women it's that 'maybe' means a variety of things, none of which is 'yes.' "

"You've learned that, huh?"

"I've also learned that in these days of women's lib and whatever, a man needs every edge he can find or steal. And since I happen to be considerably larger than you, I plan to use that advantage every chance I get."

"Are you going to turn me over your knee?" she asked interestedly.

"Don't give me ideas."

"Wouldn't think of it," Pepper drawled. "Never give the opposing side a gun; it leads to uncomfortable things. Like defeat."

"You don't like to lose?"

"Not if I can help it." She stared at him and frowned. "We seem to have digressed somewhat from the point."

"What was the point?" He kissed her again.

Pepper fought for breath and cleared her throat determinedly. "The point. Ah. This macho attempt to use your muscles—that's the point. It's unfair."

" 'All's fair in . . .' Well, you know the rest."

" 'Love and war,' if I remember correctly. And it's going to be the latter with a vengeance if you don't put me down."

Thor looked virtuous. "It was your challenge, therefore I choose the weapons. It's a rule."

"Look, I'm not used to this altitude, and I'm getting dizzy. Why don't we sit down and discuss the rules?"

Thor appeared to think about her request, then nodded, making a complicated maneuver that ended with him sitting on the couch and Pepper sitting in his lap.

"This wasn't quite what I had in mind," she noted dryly.

"It's what I had in mind. You were saying something about rules?" He seemed to find her ponytail fascinating, winding the silky hair around his hand and apparently watching light play on the silvery strands.

Or maybe, she thought wryly, he was adding insurance to the arm resting across her lap. Since he obviously didn't intend to let her escape, Pepper, characteristically, got on with the matter at hand.

But it was damnably hard to ignore the hard thighs beneath her. . . .

"The rules. Well, you said it was up to you to choose the weapons, but any contest of physical superiority ends right here."

"Oh?"

"Definitely. It's too unequal. Brute strength wins

out in the end, and we both know it," she said seriously.

He looked at her for a long moment. "That's a lesson usually learned in a hard school; my curiosity about your past is growing by leaps and bounds."

Pepper felt a peculiar little mental shock and wondered silently at his perception. But she wasn't ready to talk about hard schools or pasts, and skated over the subject lightly. "When one is pint-size, it's a lesson easily and quickly learned. So—no physical domination, okay?"

In an odd little gesture his free hand lifted to lie along the side of her neck, the thumb moving gently beneath her ear. His expression was totally and completely serious. "I'd never hurt you, Pepper. That's one thing you can always be very sure of."

Swallowing hard—for some reason there seemed to be a lump in her throat—Pepper decided to accept that for agreement. "Fine." She decided to lighten the atmosphere. "And since that washes out your strongest weapon—no wordplay intended—what do you choose instead?"

Thor's lazy smile indicated an approval of her light question, but his reply made her realize suddenly that her own strategy was marching inexorably over quicksand.

"Honesty."

"I see." She wondered where her own unwary steps had led her, and how he defined honesty. "No punches pulled. No quarter asked . . . or granted."

"You said it first." He was still smiling, but watchful now, gray eyes probing. "No quarter. No holds barred. And since honesty is the weapon"—his smile grew—"I'll be the first to employ it. Tell me something, Pepper. Were you looking for a place to park your RV for a few weeks? Or were you looking for a home for Fifi?"

"Dammit." Pepper was torn between a desire to laugh and an urge to hit him with something. "That's not a fair question!"

He shook his head reprovingly. "You can't cry foul whenever something doesn't suit you. Come on now, 'fess up! Your gauntlet was well hidden, but you were bent on challenge yesterday, weren't you?"

Pepper felt a smile tugging at her lips. This was honesty with a vengeance! "Well, since you obviously aren't taking to your heels, I'll admit that I could have found somewhere else to park the van."

"Not good enough."

"You want your pound of flesh, don't you?"

"Something like that."

"Beast."

"To the core. Well?"

"All right!" She glared at him; her expression was part mockery and part amused exasperation. "I was . . . interested. Satisfied?"

He was openly grinning now. "It'll do. Damn, you must have been *born* with a poker face; you certainly didn't give anything away yesterday. I figured you didn't have a subtle bone in your body."

"You call this subtle?" Pepper looked at him with a lifted brow. "If my fellow women found out about this, I'd be drummed out of the sisterhood."

"What sisterhood?" Thor looked puzzled.

Pepper decided that if he wanted honesty, he was going to get it. It was a tactic that, according to theory, was guaranteed to give most men nightmares, but she was intuitively certain that it was the right one with this particular man. Not total honesty, of course. There would always be guarded areas of any individual's privacy in which intrusion would neither be forgotten nor forgiven. She sighed. Oh, well, he knew that as well as she. Honesty in *intent*, though—well, that was different.

"News for you, pal," she told him with a gentle smile. "Women have always done the chasing; we just never let you guys know it. Subtle, you see. Which is why the sisterhood would disown me if this got out."

Thor stared at her for a long moment. "What have I gotten myself into?" he murmured.

"Trouble." She bit back a giggle. "With a capital *T* and a capital all the other letters too. You've opened a Pandora's box, remember."

"What about you?" The intent, probing expression in his gray eyes belied his easy smile. "Aren't you putting yourself in a vulnerable position by admitting interest so early in the—uh—game?"

"You mean, 'what price honesty'?" Too serious, she thought, and gave him a light answer. "Well, I've always paid my own fare. And, besides, it seems to me that a lot of the problems in human relationships arise out of trying to hide what's painfully obvious." She smiled a little. "I'd be an idiot to deny interest after the way I reacted to your—uh—physical response to my challenge. Wouldn't I?"

Something flickered in Thor's eyes, an expression that might have been admiration or approval—or bewilderment. When he spoke, his voice was a curious combination of all three emotions.

"I asked for honesty, but I didn't really expect it, Pepper. The closer I look at the puzzle, the bigger and more complicated it gets." Almost whimsically he added, "Are you real? Or will I wake up and find you were a dream?"

Pepper didn't delude herself into thinking that the question meant what it seemed to mean: that her honesty made her more imagined than real, something he'd needed but never expected to find. She wasn't that complacent about herself or that certain of him. So she simply answered the first question and tried to ignore the second.

"I'm real. And you'd better remember that honesty's a double-edged sword; it cuts both ways. You have to be honest too."

"And so?"

"And so . . . the chase is on. Do you feel hunted?"

He appeared to consider the question seriously. "Oddly enough, no. I suppose because I feel certain that you'd chase, but not trap. And I'd be a fool if I weren't flattered by your . . . interest."

Pepper was honestly surprised. "Why?"

Thor was clearly amused. "My ego, I guess. I've never been chased by an angel before."

Instead of taking the remark as the compliment it was obviously intended to be, Pepper was shaken by it. "Thor . . . don't put me on a pedestal. I'd lose my balance. I'd fall off."

In that moment Thor felt a curious need to reassure her. He didn't know why, but the need rose with a certainty not to be questioned. And he didn't question. He simply drew her closer, resting his chin against her hair and wrapping both arms around her. "You look like an angel," he told her quietly. "I don't expect you to be one. In fact, I wouldn't know what to do with an angel."

Pepper was surprised by his reaction to her plea, but warmed by it. She wanted him to think of her as a flesh-and-blood woman, not the china doll some men wanted her to be. A china doll was placed on a shelf and displayed proudly; it was rarely touched or even held. Pepper had discovered in the last few minutes just how much of a woman she was, and she didn't want to risk the loss of Thor touching and holding her.

Wary again of being too serious, of delving into too many unfamiliar emotions, she tried to lighten the mood. "You said something about giving me the nickel tour," she murmured, highly conscious of his big arms around her.

"It's gone up to a dime," he responded gravely. "Inflation, you know."

"Really? Well, I guess it'll be worth it."

"That remains to be seen."

"True." She made an experimental attempt to remove herself from his lap, both relieved and disappointed when he allowed her to get up. "Lead on."

Thor rose to his feet slowly and stood looking down at her for a moment. "I am flattered, you know," he said suddenly.

Pepper was deliberately obtuse. "Just because I think the tour'll be worth a dime?" she asked lightly.

"No." He touched the tip of her nose with one finger. "Because I'm being chased."

"It's early days yet," she told him wryly. "This time next week you may be running in fear of your very life."

"Somehow I don't think that's likely. In the meantime, however . . . This, ma'am, is the den. And, if you'll come this way . . ."

The house was beautiful. Downstairs was the living room, den, study, kitchen/breakfast nook, formal dining room, and one of the three bathrooms.

The rooms were spacious and airy, decorated— Pepper's discerning eye for such things told her— professionally, but with instructions to lean toward comfort rather than style. The furniture was composed of sturdy woods and comfortable cushions, nothing delicate or spindly. Colors varied from room to room, mostly earth tones brightened by greens and blues.

The study held her interest the longest, particularly since she was looking for clues to the man himself, and experience had taught her that work areas in the home offered the most insight for those who cared to look.

It was carpeted in deep brown, paneled in birch, and filled with bookshelves that were filled, in turn, with books of every type. Pepper could find no preference that would aid in her deductions, except that he seemed to have a fondness for mysteries. The huge oak desk in one corner was neat; no clutter of papers or objects to indicate that work was done there.

Two high-backed chairs were grouped with a table and reading lamp in another corner. In the center of the large room was a game table, suitable for card games or jigsaw puzzles, or whatever. It was bare.

In the remaining corner was a baby grand piano. Gleaming a velvety black, its polished surface spoke of loving care, but whether that was due to Thor or his housekeeper, Pepper couldn't tell. She touched a sparkling ivory key with one finger and wondered silently.

"You play, I gather," she said aloud.

"Indifferently. How about you?"

"When I get the chance."

"Feel free."

"Thanks; I just might take you up on that."

They left the matter there and went on with the tour. The laundry room held no interest for Pepper, but a good-size room with a door through to the garage did. It was bare except for a storage cabinet and a large deep sink, and appeared not to be in use.

"What's this?"

"In the plans it's called a mudroom."

"You don't use it for anything?"

"No. Why?"

Pepper eyed the size of the room, paying close attention to the sink. "I was just wondering . . . well, if you don't need it for anything, d'you mind if I use it while I'm here? I promise to leave it just as I found it."

Thor looked at her curiously. He wondered why she needed a large bare room, but decided that the reason would become apparent in time. "I don't mind. Help yourself."

"Thanks." Pepper smiled a little, wondering how he would react to the second invasion he would suffer shortly. She hoped it would be humorously; never before, she was reasonably sure, had a man been the victim of such an honestly declared and inwardly devious chase.

If nothing else, she thought with humor, her methods were original. She was being totally honest in her goal—permanence—and utterly absurd in her methods. One of them would win . . . or Thor would murder her, resulting in a sort of victory by default.

"Why the Mona Lisa smile?" Thor asked a bit uneasily.

"Oh—no reason. Is the tour taking us upstairs now, or shall I imagine the rest?"

"Heaven forbid. After you." He gestured for her to precede him, still wondering about that smile but lacking the nerve to ask again.

They went up the staircase in the entranceway so she could view the four bedrooms. They were accompanied by Fifi—who'd been with them from the first of the tour, and by Brutus—who'd caught up with them in the kitchen. All the bedrooms were beautifully decorated, one containing a huge king-size waterbed. There was a central bathroom opening into the hall, and another off the master bedroom.

That room itself was the largest, and possessed a tremendous oak four-poster bed that Pepper would have needed a stool to climb onto. It looked like an antique, along with the long dresser and tall chest of drawers. The room also boasted a walk-in closet, and the bathroom contained a sunken bath deep enough to satisfy a giant.

Passing up the opportunity to call him a sybarite, Pepper made only one remark. "Awfully big house for only one person," she murmured as they were going back down the stairs.

"Mmm. I like space."

She considered his reply as they went back into the den. And a glance around at the room made her remember that she'd seen few indications of "personality" in the house. No clutter or mess, which merely indicated that he was either very neat or that his housekeeper was. More surprising—and perhaps more revealing—was the lack of personal touches.

The prints and paintings throughout the house were ambiguous as to taste, mostly landscapes and seascapes. No adventurous abstracts or romantic portraits, no favored artist. There were few ornaments, and what there was seemed more the touch of a decorator than a declaration of personal taste. Where were the souvenirs of places visited? Photos of people related or known?

Pepper wondered just how often his job took him away from home. Now, she asked herself, which one of them was putting a puzzle together? She or Thor?

"Another drink?" he asked, pulling her from speculation.

"No, thanks." She slid a hand into her pocket, absently retrieving a worry-stone and beginning to "worry" it rhythmically.

Thor watched her curiously for a moment, then stepped closer and caught her wrist. "What's this?"

Realizing only then what she'd been doing, Pepper opened her hand and watched him lift the smooth stone to examine it. "It's a worry-stone," she said.

Thor turned the object in his fingers. It looked like quartz and was roughly two inches from end to end and about a quarter of an inch thick. Oval in shape and smoothly polished, it was flat on both sides and had a slight depression in one end which was, he saw, perfectly suited to be rubbed by a thumb.

He placed the stone back in her palm, his fingers lingering on hers. "Are you worried about something?"

Rather hastily Pepper slid the stone back into her pocket. "Of course not. I quit smoking a few years ago. Some people chew gum—I play with a worry-stone."

"I see." He didn't look convinced.

Pepper decided to change the subject. "Look, it's almost suppertime, according to my stomach's clock. I think I'll take advantage of those liberated tendencies you blanketed us females with and ask you to share my meal. I can bring some stuff over from the van, since your dining room's larger than mine. Or else we can go somewhere. If you're interested, that is."

"I'm interested. But why don't we just make do with whatever's in the kitchen here? Mrs. Small usually keeps the place stocked."

"Fine with me. What were you planning to have tonight?"

"A TV dinner."

Pepper lifted a brow at him. "Is that your usual fare?"

"On Mrs. Small's day off it is."

She shook her head mournfully. "It's disgraceful to reach your advanced years without being able to cook."

Thor decided to ignore the first part of her sentence. "Don't expect me to be perfect. I suppose you can cook?"

"Yes."

"Well, that was a flat answer."

"You asked a flat question," she reminded him.

"No modest disclaimers, huh?"

"We're being honest."

"So we are," Thor said.

"Will Mrs. Small mind us invading her kitchen?"

"We just won't ask her."

"Devious man."

The rest of the evening was companionable, and if they felt the undercurrents, neither mentioned it. They observed a tacit agreement not to delve any further into their sudden relationship, treading instead around lighter topics with the wariness of fencers. They talked casually about various subjects in the curious give-and-take probing of new acquaintances, neither giving much away.

What emerged was that Thor preferred blue and enjoyed football and soft pop music and hated snails, while Pepper loved the color wine-red and also enjoyed football and pop music and could take or leave snails. Both agreed that Maine was a beautiful state and that the latest best-selling novel was fascinating and that neither nervous Dobermans nor inquisitive Chihuahuas belonged in kitchens.

After a totally deadpan preparation of hot dogs and French fries by Pepper and a joint clean-up in the kitchen, a murder mystery on television topped off the evening. Thor sided with the detective while Pepper seriously defended the murderer's motivations.

Pepper firmly dissuaded him from walking out to the RV with her, refusing his offer to help in hooking up the vehicle to his electrical supply and condescending only to accept a flashlight. After a comically grave handshake she thanked him solemnly for the meal, the flashlight, and the place in which to park her van, gathered the dogs firmly to heel, and strolled off into the darkness.

A while later, as he was lying in bed and staring up at a darkness-distorted ceiling, Thor wondered how on earth such an emotional and challenging afternoon had turned into a disconcertingly calm and companionable evening. Questions floated around in his mind, their answers beyond his reach because he didn't yet know Pepper well enough to even guess.

Was her honesty as real as it seemed? Had she

indeed decided that he might be what she was looking for and, if so, how did he really feel about that? What had happened in her life to teach her that brute strength always wins in the end? Why the worry-stone? What events in her life had shaped a woman who could challenge a man with honesty and humor?

The last question occurred just as he was dropping off to sleep, and it bothered Thor more than all the others.

Why had she not invited him for a nickel tour of her own home? In fact, without being in the least rude, she had made certain that he had not seen the inside of the RV. Was it because it contained some of the pieces he needed to put the puzzle together? And while Thor was suddenly, if sleepily, consumed with an intense desire to do so, he knew that he wouldn't set foot inside the vehicle without Pepper's invitation.

The thought followed him into dreams in which distorted RVs loomed mockingly and spewed forth countless jigsaw puzzle pieces while a cowardly Doberman looked at him with panicky brown eyes, a savage Chihuahua attempted to maul him, and the maniacal laughter of Odin fell derisively on the ears of a hapless, earthbound god of thunder. . . .

Rising earlier than usual after a restless, disturbed night, Thor decided to take the coward's way out and leave home before Mrs. Small arrived for the day. He would have dearly loved to be a fly on the wall during the meeting of his housekeeper and Pepper, Brutus, and Fifi; at the same time, the thought of likely chaos sent him out of the house after a breakfast of coffee.

Feeling both guilty and amused, he fed Lucifer and then cranked the Corvette as quietly as possible, noting that Pepper's RV was hooked up to his garage and seeing no sign of the dogs. Presumably then, she was still asleep.

He'd given her a key to the house the night before and told her to treat it as her own, and her Mona Lisa smile of the day before came suddenly back to haunt him. What would he find when he returned?

Pushing the useless speculation from his mind, Thor backed the low-slung Corvette out of the driveway and headed toward town. He had errands to run, he assured himself silently. And he'd left Mrs. Small a note to explain Pepper's presence. Sort of explain anyway.

"Coward," he muttered aloud.

When Thor parked the Corvette in his driveway later that afternoon, he saw that the only difference in the appearance of his home was the presence of Mrs. Small's little VW. He felt relieved that she hadn't, apparently, quit, but wondered what kind of reception he would get from her. Steeling himself, he headed for the front door.

As the door swung inward he heard a deep-throated "Woof!" and saw Fifi disappearing in the direction of the kitchen. As he closed the door behind him, he saw Brutus sitting squarely in the middle of the entranceway and lifting a lip at him.

Thor stood staring down at the tiny dog. "Make up your mind, pal," he told Brutus calmly. "Either you accept me or you don't; we aren't going through this little charade every time we see each other."

The lip descended to cover pointed teeth, and Brutus returned the stare. Then he got up, wagged a tail, and trotted off after Fifi. Feeling mildly pleased with himself, Thor followed the canine parade.

When he reached the kitchen door, he felt tremors in the very foundation of his world. Mrs. Small was smiling. *Smiling.* And even as he watched and listened in incredulous fascination, he heard her laugh for the first time in five years. It was an odd, deep laugh, seemingly rusty from disuse, but it was definitely a laugh.

She was leaning against the refrigerator and stirring something in a large mixing bowl, unperturbed by the Doberman trying to hide behind her as she listened to Pepper's cheerful little-girl voice. And Pepper was sitting on the end of the counter wearing jeans, ridiculously small boots, and a red and black plaid shirt over a black sweater.

Thor watched her gesture to illustrate some point he wasn't taking in, wondering dimly how she had managed to pile all her hair on the top of her head to achieve that tousled, impossibly sexy look. Then she glanced toward the door and saw him, breaking the trance he seemed to be swimming in.

"Hi, Thor," she said casually.

"Hi," he managed.

She tilted her head to one side like an inquisitive robin. "Are you all right? You look strange."

"I'm fine," he murmured, deciding not to explain that he'd expected a mushroom cloud and gotten Alice's mirror instead.

He wasn't sure he understood it himself.

Four

Before another word could be spoken, a head popped out of the doorway to the hall leading to the mud and laundry rooms. It was a masculine head roughly seventeen years old, with an attempt at a mustache, fairly long brown hair, and the mild brown eyes of a hopeful spaniel.

"Jo Jo's done, Pep. Want me to start on Dickens next?"

While Thor was pondering the meaning of these mysterious words, Pepper answered cheerfully, "Give him a few more minutes to settle down; Mrs. Shannon just brought him a little while ago. I'll take care of Jo Jo while you work on Ladama's nails."

"Right." He vanished.

Pepper slid down off the counter, using every ounce of her control to keep from laughing at Thor's bewildered expression. Studiously refusing to look at him, she smiled at Mrs. Small instead. "After I've finished, I'll go and dig out that recipe, Jean. You may not be able to find all the ingredients around here, but I have most of the raw spices."

Mrs. Small nodded. "I'd love to try my hand at it."

"Great. See you later." With a wave to Thor Pepper disappeared through the doorway.

He stared after her. Jo Jo? Dickens? Ladama? He looked at Mrs. Small. *Jean?*

Cryptically Mrs. Small said, "Sukiyaki. Authentic. I'll need to borrow her wok though." She turned back to her mixing bowl with an absent "Move, Fifi." As the Doberman shifted slightly sideways and continued to regard Thor with uneasy eyes, the housekeeper added even more cryptically, "A little Japanese village."

Shaking off the growing conviction that this was a continuation of his wild dream, Thor headed purposefully for the mudroom. He didn't know what was going on in his house, but he meant to find out.

The mudroom had been transformed. Along the garage side of the wall were several wire kennels of various sizes, four of them occupied by three poodles and a cocker spaniel. On a makeshift table sat a disdainful collie whose paw was being bent over by the strange young man with the attempt at a mustache. A collection of bottles sat on the wide counter beside the sink, along with several crumpled towels and a stack of neatly folded ones.

Another table, this one entirely professional, had been set up on the other side of the sink. On shelves beneath it were three hair dryers; a variety of electric clippers, brushes, and combs; and a tasteful selection of narrow, colorful ribbons. On the top of the table stood a silver-gray miniature poodle, eyes half closed in blissful enjoyment as two brushes were worked steadily through his thick coat.

Wielding the brushes with the casual, easy precision of an expert was Pepper. She didn't look around as the door opened, but simply said firmly, "Out, Brutus."

Thor looked down to see the tiny Chihuahua turn stiffly and stalk from the room. He shut the door and leaned back against it, staring again around the room. "What the hell?" he muttered.

"Thor, this is Tim." She gestured toward the young man with the nail clippers, still without looking around. "Tim, our host."

Tim looked up briefly. "Hi." Then bent again, his full attention back on the collie's nails.

"Hi. So this is what you wanted the room for?"

"Obviously. You don't mind, do you? It's Kristen's business, you know. She had a little place in town, but since the lease was up, I decided to work out here instead."

"Does Kristen know?" Thor asked dryly.

"No. But then, she thinks she's coming back to the States."

"And she isn't?" Thor pulled fragments of conversation into his mind. "I thought you said you planned to move on in a few weeks."

Pepper glanced at him, wondering in amusement if he was beginning to feel trapped. "That's what I plan. I think Kristen will come back only to pack up her things. That English breeder had something permanent in mind when he swept her off, I just know it. They'll be happy together."

Thor pondered the information. "I see. Did you— uh—introduce them, by any chance?"

"Sort of. You don't mind about this, do you?"

A neat change of subject, he decided. "No. No, if Mrs. Small doesn't mind, then I don't."

"Jean loves dogs."

"I didn't know that," he mumbled.

"Mmm. Anyway, we'll be out of your hair within a few weeks." Pepper sent an amused glance his way. "So you don't have to panic."

"I wasn't," he told her, sending a glance toward the younger man and hoping that the conversation was too cryptic for him to follow.

"Of course not. The thought of my moving in bag and baggage doesn't daunt you a bit, does it?"

Thor decided to use one of her tricks and change the subject. "What's this about a little village in Japan and sukiyaki?"

She was blandly casual. "Just a recipe I picked up a few years ago. I'm about to turn on the clippers here, which will make conversation totally impossible. And I think Jean has your lunch ready."

Thor smiled wryly at the far from subtle hint. "Okay, okay. No help from you in the god of thunder's quest, I take it."

Pepper chose a set of clippers and plugged them into the outlet beside the table, giving Thor a limpid smile. "Fair is fair. When the quarry turns to confront his huntress . . . well, who knows?"

His smile went a little crooked. Respect for her grew as he realized that the lady was far from dumb. She saw that, however willing he was to be chased, he wasn't yet ready to explain his reasons for running. With a slight inclination of his head that was half acceptance and half salute, he murmured, "Just call you Diana."

"Goddess of the hunt?" she queried lightly,

demonstrating a knowledge of Greek as well as Norse mythology.

"Goddess of the hunt. Join me for lunch?"

She shook her head slightly. "I have to finish up my friends here before five."

"You have to eat," he reminded.

"I usually skip lunch."

"Bad habit."

"I never claimed to be perfect. See you, Thor."

Giving in to the nudge, Thor sighed softly and left the makeshift grooming parlor, hearing the clippers begin to buzz loudly.

Mrs. Small—Thor couldn't bring himself to think of her as Jean—served him cheese enchiladas, and since it wasn't her habit to experiment with "foreign" fare, he looked at her questioningly.

"Mexico," she responded in answer to the look. "Pepper's recipe. Authentic."

Thor sampled Pepper's recipe. "Delicious," he said honestly. Before Mrs. Small could return to the kitchen, he decided to do a bit of unscrupulous digging. "When was she in Mexico?" he asked casually.

"Last year." The housekeeper picked up a china vase from the sideboard and apparently decided to take it back to the kitchen for a wash rather than a dusting. "The same time as you were there."

Thor looked up quickly. "Does she know I was there?"

"Didn't mention it." She left the room.

Staring after her, Thor wondered which of them hadn't mentioned it—Pepper or Mrs. Small. His housekeeper had never struck him as the type to talk about her employer, but he wasn't sure, after today, that she wouldn't answer a direct question if Pepper asked. And he couldn't help but wonder if

Pepper had decided to do a bit of unscrupulous digging as well.

He also wondered about her presence in Mexico. Clearly the lady had done a bit of traveling; the recipes from Japan and Mexico, and she'd mentioned spending six months in a desert with camels. Not that she'd put it that way, of course, but *desert* and *camels* suggested Arabia or northern Africa, both of which he, too, had spent time in.

She hadn't traveled the world grooming dogs, he knew. So what *did* she do? Was she wealthy? Heaven knew she neither looked nor acted it, but he'd quickly learned not to stick any kind of label on Pepper, and that RV hadn't come cheap.

It was another piece to the puzzle and he didn't know where to fit it.

Five o'clock had just passed when the last of the dogs had been picked up by admiring owners and Tim had left with the girlfriend who'd come to get him. Pepper finished cleaning up the mudroom, leaving it neat before wandering out into the kitchen. An appetizing scent led her to the oven, where she discovered lasagna bubbling away.

Pepper grinned faintly, noting that the lasagna recipe and the ones for cheese enchiladas and sukiyaki were tacked to a small cork board above a counter work area. She hoped that Thor didn't mind this culinary experimentation, since Jean seemed determined to try every recipe in Pepper's rather crowded recipe box.

Still smiling, she left the kitchen. Both Thor and Jean had told her to treat the house as home, and she felt no uneasiness about doing just that.

Besides, she had to find the pets; they seemed to have disappeared in the last few hours.

The muffled roar of the vacuum cleaner told her that Jean was finishing up the bedrooms upstairs, but no other sound led her to the pets or Thor. Puzzled, she went from room to room, ending up in the empty study. Nothing. She crossed to the window with a view of the pasture, pulled the heavy drapes aside and looked through.

And she couldn't help but grin.

Fifi sat off to one side, wary and keeping her distance as she watched Thor throwing a small stick for Brutus to fetch. The difference in size of Thor's six-feet-three two-hundred-pound frame and Brutus's seven inches and less than two pounds was utterly ridiculous. But both seemed oblivious to the comical aspects of their game.

Pepper watched for a few moments, then rose on her tiptoes to look down toward the hollow and Lucifer's stable. The bottom half of the Dutch door was closed, she saw, and the stallion shut inside. So . . . Thor really was worried about his horse hurting the dogs. She'd have to do something about that. Tomorrow. Maybe before Thor woke up in the morning.

Pleased that Thor was making an effort to get friendly with her pets, but wondering if it was only because he wanted to save wear and tear on his nerves, she turned away from the window. The baby grand in the room drew her like a magnet, and she went over to sit on the padded bench.

Her fingers moved over the keys lightly, fluidly. She played a bit of Mozart from memory, then began a soft pop song that was a favorite of hers. The piano was beautifully tuned, and Pepper lost herself in the enjoyment of having the chance to play. Leaving her piano behind was the one sacrifice she'd had to make in launching her gypsy life-style.

The words to the song formed in her mind, her throat, and she allowed them to escape softly. Only then did she realize that it was a love song about a woman who loved beyond all reason and feared to lose that love. It wasn't a sad song, oddly enough, but one filled with determination. And, even as she was singing, Pepper wondered in amusement at the proddings of her subconscious.

The last notes trailed away into silence, and the sudden sound of a husky masculine voice threw her into confusion for one of the few times in her life.

"Was that meant for me?"

Startled, she swung around on the bench. Thor was standing in the doorway, leaning back against the jamb with his arms crossed over his broad chest, and something in his eyes made her almost too breathless to answer.

"I thought you were outside," she managed to say after a few moments of silence.

"Ah. Then it wasn't meant for me?"

He wasn't going to let her avoid answering, dammit. "I thought you were outside, I told you. The song was for me. I don't like advertising my lack of voice."

"Fishing?" he inquired with a lifted brow.

Pepper was honestly surprised. "Of course not."

"Then," he told her calmly, "you don't know ability when you hear it. You could sing professionally."

She blinked at him. "I could? Uh . . . I question your taste, but thank you for the compliment."

"You play beautifully too."

"Thank you," she said gravely, staring at him.

"And you look sexy as hell with your hair piled on top of your head like that. I meant to tell you earlier."

She blinked again. "You're feeling *very* complimentary" was all she was able to say.

"I'm also feeling unusually protective," he said conversationally. "So I guess I'd better know how you feel about that. I mean, do you object to my feeling protective, or is that one of the qualities you're looking for?"

"Would it matter?" she asked in sudden amusement, assuming that eventually he'd get around to the real point he wanted to make.

He considered her question. "I doubt it. I don't seem to be able to control it. However, if you object—women's lib or whatever—then I'll see what I can do about it. *Do* you object?"

"Not really. As long as it isn't taken to extremes. I mean, if you accept that I'm not helpless, we'll get along fine."

"I accept that."

"Wonderful. And so?"

"What kind of heat does that RV have?"

The point? she wondered. "I have a kerosene heater. Why?"

Thor frowned. "I don't like that."

"They're perfectly safe," she offered, still amused.

"I suppose. But . . . there's a cold front moving through tonight, and I won't sleep a wink. Why don't you move into the house?"

Ah. The point. Pepper bit back a giggle. "You take your time in getting around to the point, don't you?"

"I'm serious," he scolded, but there was a grin working at his mouth.

"What brought this on?" she asked dryly.

"It's getting chilly outside, and I wondered. I could be callous and say that I don't want my house burning down along with your RV, but that didn't occur to me until just now. Actually it's you and the mutts I'm worried about. Humor me. Move your things in here."

"Thor—"

"God knows, there's enough space. Pick any of the bedrooms—I won't even exclude mine. I won't even charge you rent. Just keep giving Mrs. Small those wonderful recipes and sing for me from time to time."

"Thor—" she tried again, but he cut her off once more.

"The mutts too. If you feel obligated or something, we'll work out a fair trade of services. I mean—uh, no, I didn't mean that the way it sounded. I'll make you wash dishes or something. . . ."

Pepper was laughing.

"That object you see protruding from my mouth," he told her ruefully, "is my foot. Be gentle with me; I've never asked a woman to live with me before."

She choked off a last laugh. "You haven't, huh? I never would have guessed. I think your ulterior motives are showing."

"Bite your tongue. I'm trying to be gallant."

"With the accent on the last syllable?"

"Right. Chivalrous," he said.

"It also means flirtatious."

"Just so, Diana."

"Mmm." Pepper stared at him. "Let's fall back on

honesty, shall we? Thor, do you know what you're doing?"

"You think I'm being reckless?"

"Suicidally reckless. If you're counting on the home-team advantage, I should warn you in all fairness that I never need a cheering section."

Thor started to laugh. "You know, whenever we're together, the metaphors fly so thick and fast that I can barely keep up. Cheering section? I thought this challenge was just between you and me."

"You know what I mean."

"It's scary to admit it, but yes, I think I do."

"Why scary?"

"You're beginning to make sense to me; that'd scare any sane man."

"Thanks a lot."

"You're welcome. And we're digressing again. Will you move in?"

Abruptly serious, she asked slowly, "Do you really think that would be a good idea?"

He nodded, still smiling but clearly serious. "Yes. We've got—what?—a few weeks before you either catch me or fold up your RV and steal away. We should make the most of that time."

Pepper felt a smile tugging at her lips. "You really do like the idea of being chased, don't you?"

"I told you, it panders to my ego," he returned solemnly, and then relented because of the suspicious look on her face. "Okay, okay. It may be unmacho to admit it, but yes, I'm getting a hell of a kick out of the whole thing. Although I haven't seen any real evidence of chasing yet."

"Haven't you?" she murmured with another Mona Lisa smile.

He stared at her. "Am I being manipulated?" he demanded suddenly.

She gave him a "Who, me?" look of innocence.

"I think I am," he told the ceiling in mock despair. "And I thought it was all my idea."

"But it was," she told him gently. "That's the subtlety of it."

"You're dangerous."

Pepper started laughing, unable to keep a straight face after his look of sham horror. "I've been told that before. But in this case I'll confess that I hadn't planned on moving into your house. That's a bit too blatant even for my taste."

"I'm glad you admitted that. Honesty I can deal with, but subtlety unnerves me."

"I'll keep that in mind."

"Do that. Are you moving in?"

"Thor—"

"Humor me."

She stared into his smiling gray eyes. "If you'll accept a promise from me," she said seriously.

"What are you promising?"

"I'm promising not to complicate your life—more than you can stand anyway. And I'm promising that you won't have to tell me to go. If you get tired of the game"—she smiled slightly—"or take to your heels in earnest, I'll know. I want you to understand that you won't have to ask me to leave."

Gazing at her, Thor realized dimly that this was the first time either of them had admitted that the game would have an ending, and that it might not be a happy one. "Are you moving in?" he repeated steadily.

"Are you accepting the promise?"

"If I have to," he said unwillingly.

"You do."

"All right then." Thor shook his head. "This is the strangest chase I've ever heard of. Why aren't you attacking me and tearing my clothes off?" he demanded mournfully.

Approving of the brighter atmosphere, she said reprovingly, "That's what happens when I catch you."

"Then why the hell am I running?" he demanded in bewilderment.

They stared at each other for a moment, then both burst out laughing.

"Tuck away your gallant manners, will you?"

"I just offered to help."

"Thor, I'm bringing over some clothes and that's all. They won't be heavy and I can manage nicely on my own, thank you very much."

"You might trip in the dark."

"Thor."

"Why don't you just admit that you don't want me in your RV and be done with it?"

She was slipping, Pepper decided, if it was as obvious as all that. She turned and leaned back against the closed front door, staring up at Thor. He wanted honesty, she reminded herself. "All right then. I don't want you in the van."

"Thanks a lot."

"Sorry."

"Afraid I'll steal the silver?"

"None to steal."

"Afraid I'll find puzzle pieces?" he asked more seriously.

His perception caught her off guard, and for a moment she was silent. Without realizing that she was doing it, Pepper reached into a pocket of her jeans and brought out the ever-present worry-stone, her thumb moving rhythmically in the depression. "Every time we turn around," she murmured, "we seem to be stumbling over honesty."

Thor noticed her unconscious gesture, but didn't comment on it. "That's a good thing to stumble over," he said instead.

She nodded slightly. "As long as one of us doesn't fall." Before he could respond, she was going on evenly. "Okay, then. I came into your home, Thor. And I looked for clues."

"To me?"

"To you. I found a beautiful house. I didn't find clues. I didn't find you."

"I see." He gazed at her steadily. "But I'd find you in the van?" When she hesitated, he said flatly, "I won't step inside the door without your permission, Pepper. I promise you that."

She nodded again and said almost unwillingly, "You'd find me, I think. I've never looked at myself the way you do—pieces of a puzzle, I mean. But if that's what I am, then all the pieces are there. That van is my . . . anchor. My lifeline. Something to come back to. Someplace to store memories. Home. I believe that everything I am is in that van."

Thor took a deep breath and released it slowly. He reached out a hand, grasping hers and stilling the busy thumb. "I won't go inside without your invitation," he told her, rewording his earlier promise.

Pepper looked up at him, the honesty in her violet eyes neither a weapon nor a plea, but a simple frankness, a calm integrity that brushed aside games and left only truth. "If I ask you, it'll be because I want you to see me. With no veils, no shields, nothing hidden. I'll want you to see everything that I am. Do you understand what that will mean?"

His hand tightened around hers. He bent suddenly and kissed her briefly, a kiss that was curiously rough, almost a protest against what couldn't be denied. "Yes. I know what it will mean." His gray eyes were almost violently stormy, his voice taut.

She pulled her hand from his slowly, still unaware of the worry-stone as she slipped it into her pocket automatically. "Shall I get my things?" she asked him quietly.

"Get your things." As she turned to open the door he added, "Pepper . . . no matter what happens between us, I want you to remember something. You have valid reasons for your rules. I have valid reasons for mine."

She paused to look back at him, alarmed by the raw sound of his voice. What had they begun? What had they unleashed that had the power to disturb them both this way? Whatever it was, the intensity of it frightened her. "I almost wish . . . I hadn't challenged you," she told him, and she had never been more honest.

His smile was tight. "I almost wish I hadn't accepted your challenge. But I think we both know there's no going back now."

"Yes. That's what frightens me." She went out, closing the door softly behind her.

"It frightens me too," he murmured, staring at the door's carved panel as if it offered answers. "Dammit to hell, Pepper, why can't I tell you to leave?"

Coming back up the walk a few minutes later, Pepper glanced in the den window, where the drapes had yet to be drawn. She saw Thor sitting in a chair before a newly kindled fire, with Fifi sitting at his feet. The Doberman's long, aristocratic face was turned toward him, her chin on his knee as he pulled absently and rhythmically at her small pointed ears.

Pepper smiled at the dog's acceptance of Thor, but then she got a look at his brooding face, and her smile died. She stood for a moment, looking in and ignoring the breeze that had turned to a chill wind.

Whatever was building between her and Thor, it was happening too fast. They barely knew each other. It had to slow down, she thought desperately. If the headlong rush continued, it would stop only with a painful impact, injuring one or both of them beyond time's ability to heal.

It had not been a part of her plans, she thought dimly, this wrenching of the senses and the heart. She had thought love a warm and gentle emotion, not something that left senses bewildered and unfulfilled bodies aching long into the night. Not something that hurt and frightened. For the first time in her life she wanted to run away.

But she couldn't.

Pepper squared her shoulders and continued up the walk to the front door. Light, she reminded herself. Keep it light. No more soul-searching. Whatever is happening you obviously can't control. So don't look back, and don't look ahead. Light your candles one at a time, and just keep going, dammit.

It was good advice.

She only hoped she could follow it.

Carrying an armful of clothes and with a heavy duffel bag slung over her shoulder, she closed the front door behind her with a thud, not surprised to see that Thor was already in the entranceway.

"Here, let me," he said, reaching out to slip the bag off her shoulder.

Pepper let it go with relief. "Thanks. It's heavier than I thought." She nodded at Fifi, who was standing at heel by his side. "I see you've made a conquest."

Thor looked down in surprise, having obviously been unaware of Fifi's presence. "So I have."

"I hope you're prepared for her to dog your steps—no pun intended."

He winced. "I'm glad that was unintentional; it's a lousy pun."

"So what do you expect at nine o'clock at night after a delicious meal of lasagna and three glasses of wine?" she asked practically, beginning to climb the stairs and relieved that he'd followed her light lead.

"Better puns. You did say you wanted the waterbed, didn't you?"

Pepper turned in the appropriate door and flipped the light switch. "Can't you tell?" she asked casually, dumping the armful of clothes down on the bright orange comforter.

Thor halted in the doorway, staring at Brutus. The little dog was lying calmly in the center of the bed, front legs crossed and big eyes blinking sleepily in the light. "How did he know?" Thor asked blankly.

"Experience." Pepper laughed. "When I visit friends here in the States, he usually goes with me. And if there's a waterbed, that's where I sleep."

Shaking his head, Thor set the duffel bag on a chair by the door. "Don't tell me Fifi will expect to sleep with me?" he asked uneasily.

"Not unless you invite her to," Pepper answered solemnly. "She's a lady."

"Cute."

"I'm serious. She won't come up on the bed unless you call her. Not while you're awake anyway."

"Great." Thor sighed, looking down at the large dog sitting patiently at his side. Then he looked back at Pepper, his eyes restless. "Do you play chess?" he asked abruptly.

"Yes," she replied, surprised.

"Then how about a game? If you're not too tired, that is."

All of Pepper's instincts told her to turn in early and let the night and sleep take the edge off tension, although she didn't think they would. But there was a faint, almost unwilling plea in Thor's eyes, and she couldn't ignore it. "Sure. I'd like to take a shower first though."

He looked relieved. "Same here. But I have to go turn Lucifer out of his stall first; he hates being shut up all night. So I'll meet you downstairs in about an hour?"

"Fine."

She watched him wave with apparent cheerfulness and head back downstairs, Fifi at his heels. Absently hoping he'd remember to leave the dog inside, she searched through the jumble of clothing on the bed until she'd found her robe, then went into the bathroom adjoining her new bedroom.

Habit born of spending a great deal of time in an RV with a small water tank made her shower brief. She dried off quickly, then donned the floor-length velour robe, zipping the front up to the base of her throat. It was sapphire in color and had heavy batwing sleeves. It was not, she thought judiciously, a seductive garment, and that seemed perfect at the moment. Looking from the inside out, Pepper never realized that the enveloping garment lent her a tiny, rather fragile appearance; an appearance that some men would find far more sexy than bare limbs and cleavage.

She took down her hair and brushed the silvery strands; then, after a moment's hesitation, put it back up and studied the effect in the slightly fogged mirror over the vanity. Odd. Thor had called the hairstyle sexy. Dispassionate scrutiny convinced Pepper that she looked like a dolled-up Pekingese.

Shaking her head in bemusement, she left the bathroom. Five minutes and an upended duffel bag located her slippers, and then she headed downstairs. She heard Thor whistling in his bedroom as she went down the hall. Well, at least he sounded cheerful, she noted with amusement.

Pepper went into the den and knelt in the deep-pile carpet before the blazing fire. Watching the flames leaping, she followed her own advice about avoiding soul-searching. Instead, she looked as objectively as possible, at the behavior of her and Thor since her "challenge."

"We pretend it's a game," she realized slowly, speaking aloud in the quiet room. "We pretend . . . and we drag in metaphors and puns, and toss the challenge back and forth. . . ." And then, she also realized, something real pulled at them. And they faced each other in an unguarded, off-center moment filled with an intensity both wanted to back away from. In those moments lurked the danger.

No wonder laughter inevitably followed those

moments, she thought ruefully. That intensity scared the hell out of both of them, and laughter was a natural channel for fear.

Pepper was under no illusions as to the traditional belief that men walked boldly into danger. Most walked boldly, certainly, but few went unafraid. There wasn't *that* much difference between the sexes. Unfortunately and unfairly, men were trained by environment, heredity, and too many generations of being "strong and silent" to present a fearless face to the world.

She shook her head at the follies of trapping people into roles, then bit back an ironic laugh as she remembered that both she and Thor were playing roles they'd shaped for themselves. Games. And she wondered which fact they would face first: that they were playing a game—or that it wasn't a game at all.

A sudden sound brought her head up sharply, and Pepper frowned as she listened intently. It had sounded like a muffled howl, she thought. What on earth. . . ?

With only that warning and an instinctive knowledge of what might have happened, Pepper barely had time to prepare herself for a hundred-pound Doberman, soaking wet and quivering with anxiety, bounding into her lap.

"Oh, Fifi," she murmured unsteadily. "You didn't."

"She sure as hell did!" Thor announced irately from the doorway.

Five

Holding Fifi with both arms and absently aware of the water soaking the front of her robe, Pepper stared at the doorway. Thor stood there, dripping, with only a towel knotted at his lean waist.

And the towel was slipping.

Being a graduate of a California university and having been a traveler for years, Pepper had viewed men in various stages of undress. She'd seen men on beaches wearing little more than moral support, and a curious visit to one rather infamous night spot in Europe had boasted a star attraction who'd scorned even that minimal covering. If she'd felt anything on such occasions, it had been a mild analytical interest. In her opinion most men—like most women—looked better with a judicious draping of material here and there.

But Thor's towel seemed to her a sinful crime against nature.

Impressive with his clothes on, he was far more so without them. Powerfully muscled without being overly so, he was deeply tanned, and there wasn't a spare ounce of fat on his large frame. The thick mat of hair on his broad chest was gold, arrowing down his flat stomach to disappear beneath the towel. And the hands-on-hips glaring stance prompted an image of a virile god of thunder.

Pepper's mouth was suddenly dry, and her ability to breathe easily seemed impaired. With a wrenching effort she tore her eyes away to look down at the trembling dog in her lap. She was very grateful that Thor was too angry to pick up the tremulous desire within her.

"Why didn't you warn me?" he was demanding.

"Sorry." She was also grateful for the amusement warring with awareness inside of her. "Uh . . . Fifi likes communal showers. I forgot."

"I'll bet." Thor hitched absently at the towel.

Pepper looked hastily away again. "I swear. Look, you go finish your shower in peace while I dry her off. You're—uh—dripping all over the carpet." She cursed the last sentence silently as he looked down and seemed to become aware of how he was dressed. Or not dressed. And when he gazed at her again—she couldn't seem to stop staring at him—she could see the sudden awareness in his eyes.

"Pepper . . ."

Damn, she thought. Oh, damn, how are we ever going to get to know each other with this . . . this combustion between us? Heaving Fifi off her lap with a strength born of desperation, she got up quickly and grasped the dog's collar. "I'll just go and—" She broke off abruptly and made tracks for the makeshift grooming parlor and the towels used for her canine clients.

Thor stared after her for a moment, then cursed softly and headed for the bathroom upstairs to finish his interrupted shower.

By the time Pepper got Fifi dry and calm again, a glance at her robe told her that she had suffered quite a bit in the dog's wet retreat. The sapphire velour was clinging to the curves beneath it, the material too wet for a hasty drying. She swore under her breath, ordered her pet to stay in the den, and went back upstairs to her bedroom.

It wasn't so much *finding* another robe as choosing between those she had, and the choice took a few moments. Out-and-out seduction had never been a part of her plans, and the last thing she wanted tonight was to spark the highly combustible feelings between her and Thor. But since she liked the gliding feel of silk next to her flesh even in winter, her nighttime wardrobe was somewhat limited in the area of concealment.

She finally chose a violet silk nightgown a bit less transparent than the others available. It was floor-length with spagetti straps and a moderate V-neckline, the material slightly gathered beneath her breasts. Over it she donned a matching negligee with a tie closing and long sleeves with wide cuffs at the wrists.

Pepper returned to the study ahead of Thor, and was frowning down at Fifi when he entered the room.

"I'll get the chessboard and set it up on the coffee table in front of the fire—" he began as he came in, but he broke off abruptly. His eyes glided over her new outfit as he automatically finished turning back the cuffs of his blue-and-black plaid flannel shirt.

"Instead of that," she said casually, moving away from the fire's golden light and making a mental note not to stand there again in a silk nightgown, dammit, "if you have a deck of playing cards somewhere around, why don't we try a few hands of poker? It's a little late to start a chess game."

"Poker," he murmured abstractedly. He shook his head, obviously to rid himself of another thought, since his next words were agreement. "Okay. There's a new deck and some chips in the study. While we're at it, we might as well finish off that wine. Why don't you get the wine and glasses while I get the cards?" Before she could respond, he was out of the room.

Pepper silently went to fetch the wine. She didn't suspect Thor of trying to deprive her of inhibitions, since she'd told him at dinner that her head was as hard as her cast-iron stomach and that the only effect wine had on her was to sharpen her wits. And since she liked wine, she had no argument with his suggestion.

A few moments later both were seated on the floor on either side of the coffee table, Thor leaning back against a chair and Pepper against the couch. Their wineglasses were at their elbows, and Thor was opening a new deck of cards.

Pepper glanced down at Fifi, where the still-nervous dog lay beside her, and couldn't help but laugh. "You've lost ground; the poor girl was frightened half to death by that bellow of yours."

Thor followed her gaze and grinned ruefully. "Her sudden entrance into my shower didn't do me much good, either. She just barged right in. I thought you said she was a lady!"

"Only where her sleeping habits are concerned."

Shooting a quick look across the table, Thor half opened his mouth to comment, then apparently thought better of it.

Dryly Pepper said, "No need to be discreet; that's one unasked question I'll answer."

"What did I hesitate to ask?"

"If Fifi's owner shared the—uh—same trait?" Pepper asked with a grin.

"Sharp, aren't you?"

"I try. To answer: yes."

"A lady . . . but only where sleeping habits are concerned?"

"If you accept the traditional definition of lady-like behavior."

"Now you've got me curious."

"Good."

"No elaboration?"

"Oh, I don't think so. I think I'll just cut bait. You should be nicely hooked by now."

Thor started to laugh. "Dammit, Pepper!"

"Honesty's a wonderful thing, isn't it? What stakes shall we play for?"

"Sky's the limit. Shall I bet my house?"

"Better not."

"Are you challenging me again?"

"In spades . . . if you'll forgive another bad pun."

"I won't forgive that one. Cut for the deal?"

"Right."

"Ten of clubs."

"Queen of hearts. I deal." Pepper began to shuffle the deck. "I hope you can afford to drop a bundle," she told him demurely. Briskly, skillfully, slender fingers flying, she dealt the hand.

Thor leaned his elbows on the low table and

stared across at her. "I think I should have held out for chess."

Pepper picked up her cards. "Bet."

He sighed and pushed a couple of chips to the center of the table. "Sky's the limit, I said. Why do I get the feeling I'll regret it?"

Nearly two hours and quite a few hands later, Thor laid down a straight and stared at Pepper. "Well, go ahead—I know you'll beat it."

She laid down a full house, aces over queens, and grinned as she raked in the pile of chips to add to her considerable winnings.

"Damn, you're good."

Pepper smiled and slid two fingers beneath the tight cuff of her negligee, removing an ace of hearts from its hiding place. With a professional snap, the card landed in front of Thor.

"I also cheat," she told him placidly. "Not ladylike at all."

"Damn," he repeated blankly, staring down at the card and then at her. "When did you swipe it?"

"While I was dealing."

"I watched your hands," he protested.

"Mmm. I learned from the best."

"Don't tell me. Monte Carlo?"

"Actually no. They knew him in Monte Carlo; he couldn't play there."

Thor groaned. "You're a cardsharp!"

"Has a nice, dishonest ring to it, doesn't it?"

"Your checkered past."

"You're fishing now."

"With every line I can find. Look, d'you mind furnishing just one small piece of the puzzle gratis? I'm stumbling around in the dark here."

Pepper felt a tiny mental shock as his imagery matched her own. Stumbling in the dark? Aware now of what happened in these off-center, unguarded moments, she could literally see the clear-cut limits of their roles becoming hazy. She picked up her glass, sipping the cool wine and wondering despairingly why she had to constantly wave puzzle pieces at him in challenge.

"Off the top of my head, or d'you want to ask a question?" she heard herself ask abruptly.

"Question."

"Time out for a question from the peanut gallery," she mocked lightly.

"Cute."

"Well. Fair trade then. If I answer your question, you have to answer mine."

"All right," he said slowly.

"So ask."

"An honest answer?"

"If I can."

"Pepper—"

"All right! An honest answer."

Thor reached a hand across to cover the restless fingers worrying her wineglass. His thumb swept lightly across a long, thin scar across the back of her hand. "How did that happen?"

Surprised, Pepper looked down at the scar for a moment and then back at him. "Oh. That."

"Uh-huh."

She frowned at him. "I could say I fell down on something when I was three."

"You could. It might even be true. Is it?"

Pepper sighed. She didn't want to appear mysterious, but unless she supplied several of the puzzle pieces, that was probably the way her answer would sound. Still . . . he'd asked. And she'd promised to answer.

"I was cut."

"How?"

"That's two questions," she said evasively.

"No, it isn't. I asked *how* that happened; you just told me *what* happened."

"You're splitting hairs."

"Pepper."

"Oh, all right." She pulled her hand from beneath his and stared across at him. "I was cut with a knife."

It was Thor's turn to frown. "An accident?" He'd noted that she hadn't said she cut herself.

"You could say that," Pepper drawled. "I certainly didn't mean for it to happen."

"Worser and worser," he muttered. "And you still haven't told me how it happened."

She took a deep breath. "Someone wanted to take something away from me."

"A mugger?" he guessed.

Pepper hesitated for a split second. "Close enough."

"Pepper—"

"My turn," she said hastily.

"Dammit. All right, what's your question?"

She nodded toward the small scar above his left eye. "How'd you get that?"

"What?"

Pepper reached across the low table to touch the scar lightly with her fingertip. "That." And was disconcerted when he immediately caught and held her hand. She wondered why she had the odd feeling that he'd known what she was referring to; why she thought that he'd wanted her to touch him. Wishful thinking?

Thor chuckled softly. "Believe it or not, I *did* fall—out of a tree when I was seven."

Pepper started to laugh. "It figures!"

He was smiling, but he didn't laugh with her. Instead, he watched her with eyes gone a curiously metallic silver. "You and your damn rules," he said softly.

She felt his hand tighten around hers, her own amusement fading. The tingling awareness within her grew and spread with the suddenness of a brushfire. She heard her own voice, husky and unsteady, and wished that she'd shown sense and turned in early. "I warned you."

"You warned me. Sporting of you. Diana, goddess of the hunt, dropping me into a maze and turning loose her hounds. And such strange hounds." He sent an oddly expressionless glance toward Fifi. "A neurotic Doberman and an attack-trained Chihuahua."

"You didn't have to accept the challenge," she reminded him.

"Oh, but I did," he told her abruptly. "It was like waving a red cape at a bull to force an instinctive reaction."

"I can still leave," she said, after swallowing the lump in her throat.

Thor released her hand and leaned back against the chair, folding his arms across his chest. "No, you can't. We both know that. One way or another, the game has to finish. But what happens to the loser, Pepper?"

"That . . . depends on who loses."

"I know what happens if I lose. What happens if you do?"

Pepper saw where his thoughts had headed, and the ease of her understanding startled her; it was as though they were attuned somehow. They both understood that if she lost, it would be because she'd broken her rules and accepted his—a short-term relationship with no strings and no promises. And she understood then that Thor had realized she could be hurt by that.

She smiled faintly. "If I lose, I'll just drive off into the sunset. Remember what I promised. You won't have to ask me to leave."

"Dammit, Pepper," he said roughly.

She got to her feet, looking down at him and still smiling. "Don't worry about me, Thor. I'm a survivor. And I'm always ready to pay the price for any chance I take."

He was suddenly up and around the low table, catching her shoulders and looking down at her probingly. "How many times have you paid a price for taking a chance?" he demanded. "The scar on your hand—was that a price, Pepper?"

She shook her head, trying not to be so stingingly aware of his touch. "No, not really. The end result of taking a chance, I suppose, but—dammit, don't box me in!"

"What d'you think you're doing to me?" His voice was fierce. "Hell, Pepper, every time I turn around, there's a wall! I don't want to get involved with you, but I can't seem to help myself. I want to know everything there is to know about you. I want to get inside that puzzle that passes for your mind. Dammit, I want to carry you upstairs and make love to you, and that scares the hell out of me because I don't think I'd ever be able to forget you after that. I don't think I'll be able to forget you anyway. . . ."

"Do you want to forget me so badly?" she asked unsteadily, staring up at him and nearly hypnotized by the nerve pulsing erratically beside his mouth.

"I have to," he breathed huskily. "Dammit, I have

to . . . but I don't think I'll be able to. . . . God, Pepper, what're you doing to me?"

Before Pepper could answer that unanswerable question, he pulled her abruptly against him, his hands sliding over the cool silk covering her back, and sought her lips hungrily. Hunger, a strange, soul-deep hunger welling up inside of him had taken control, and Thor could no more fight it than he could ignore it.

She was on fire and weightless again, some distant part of her mind aware that he'd picked her up and placed her on the couch; another more primitive part of her mind was aware of the unfamiliar weight of his body lying half on hers. He was heavy, and she absorbed the weight of him in wonder; it should have been uncomfortable, but it wasn't. It felt right.

It didn't occur to Pepper to resist, and even if it had, her body's desires would have overwhelmed logic. As it was, both her mind and body seemed to have become two strangely disconnected things. Her mind was hazy, floating like a leaf in a fast-moving stream; her body was being bombarded by sensations it had never experienced before, and all her nerve endings seemed to have short-circuited.

She felt his fingers fumbling blindly with the tie closing of her negligee, pushing the silk aside to find the lace and silk of her gown's V-neckline. His lips followed the fiery brush of his fingers, exploring the lightly tanned flesh above the edging of lace. One of his hands rested on the back of her neck, the fingers moving in her hair; the other hand moved with rough gentleness to cup a throbbing breast warmly.

Her own fingers tightened in his hair, then loosened and moved down to grip his shoulders.

Mindlessly her head tilted back against the hand holding it. Eyes fiercely closed, she wondered hazily if this was love, knowing somehow that it was. She wanted more of him than she could ever have, needed more than he could or would give to her. And the sadness of that brought the sting of tears to her eyes and pulled her wayward mind back into her aching body.

"Sweet," he was murmuring hoarsely against her skin. "God, you're so sweet! Don't stop me, Pepper. . . ."

"I won't," she breathed unevenly, realizing only then what she was saying, realizing that he would know too. She'd told him that lovemaking for her would mean that she'd found—or believed she'd found—what she'd been looking for in a man. And it was too soon, far too soon, to tell him that, but it was true, and she was too honest to pretend.

His head lifted, and Pepper saw slate-gray eyes staring down at her, cloudy, oddly uncertain. Pepper touched his face with hands that were shaking a little, giving him the honesty he'd demanded—and now wished she could consign to hell.

"I can't ask you to stop. I don't want to, Thor."

Thor gazed into the bottomless pools of her violet eyes, seeing the shine of tears that only a part of him understood. And a frustration greater than any he'd ever known gnawed at him relentlessly. He heard what she was telling him—and he wasn't ready either to break his own rules or to ask her to break hers.

Stalemate.

Pepper knew his decision almost the moment he made it, knew that he was going to leave her. He was running, and she still didn't know why.

He got to his feet slowly and stood for a moment

looking down at her, his face taut and eyes restless. Then, with a smothered sound that might
have been a curse, he turned on his heel and
started for the front door.

She didn't try to call him back. Sitting up, she
saw him grab a jacket from the brass coat tree in
the entranceway and heard the door close quietly.
She waited for long, tense moments, but there was
no roar from the Corvette.

Pepper swung her legs off the couch and got up,
bending over the coffee table long enough to stack
the cards neatly and place the chips back in their
caddy. Then she picked up their wineglasses and
carried them to the kitchen before going silently
upstairs to her room.

The Doberman had followed her, but hesitated
in the doorway to the room, whining softly. Pepper
looked down at her for a moment, then smiled
wryly. "You too, eh? Come on in, girl. I won't close
the door all the way. You can go to him when he
comes in." Fifi lay down in front of the chair by the
door, still whimpering.

Pepper moved about the room for a few
moments, putting her clothes away neatly and
wondering if she'd be packing them back up
tomorrow. Oddly enough she didn't believe that
Thor wanted her to leave. She'd seen the conflict in
his eyes tonight, and knew that something—
perhaps his own set of rules, or something else—
was having a tug of war within him.

She had to wait and find out what . . . or who
. . . would win.

Going to the window to draw the drapes, she
automatically looked out and down, seeing the
moonlit shapes of Thor and his stallion by the fence.
She gazed out for a moment, then drew the

drapes. She slid between the sheets of the wide bed, pulling the quilted comforter up and reaching to turn out the lamp on the nightstand.

The water moved gently beneath her for a few seconds as she got comfortable and Brutus moved to his accustomed place near her feet. Then everything was still and quiet.

She didn't think she'd sleep. Her body was aching as if she were coming down with the flu, and her mind was, for once, too weary to tear apart the events of the evening, analyze them, and try to make sense of it all. The only thing she was certain of was that time seemed to have slowed to a crawl, and she'd lived a whole emotional lifetime in a little more than two days. . . .

She slept, and she dreamed, oddly, of the occasion during which she had acquired the scar that seemed to fascinate Thor. In the dream she was running through the narrow streets of London, fog hampering her sense of direction, tensely conscious of the pounding footsteps of the man chasing her. Her good hand gripped the briefcase; the cut hand had been bound on the run with a handkerchief and was throbbing with every step. And then she rounded a corner and it was all right, doubly all right, because there was a bobby and there was the house, she recognized that peculiar gate, and she could finally stop running, and damned if she'd ever carry gems again. . . .

Pepper woke with a start to see dawn's gray light creeping through the narrow crack in the drapes. Her eyelids felt scratchy, sure evidence of a restless night. And she'd moved all the way to the other side of the bed, which was easy to do on a waterbed but was, she noted, further evidence of disturbed sleep. The house was silent, and Brutus was sitting up and looking at her expectantly, his tail thudding softly against the comforter and saying "Out."

Within a few minutes Pepper was up and dressed in jeans and a thick, bulky sweater of pale pink. She splashed water on her face in the bathroom, noting the red-rimmed eyes and realizing wryly that she looked as though she'd sobbed her heart out during the night. She hadn't, of course; that was just the way she inevitably looked after a bad night.

She brushed her hair and left it to fall, straight and shining, past her waist, then donned her suede ankle boots, tucked Brutus under an arm, and quietly went downstairs. Fifi joined them just as she opened the front door, and she took a moment to reflect that Thor, too, had left his bedroom door ajar so the dog could get in.

Standing on the front porch, she watched the dogs race around in the chill morning air for a while, sharply calling both to heel when she heard Lucifer gallop up to the fence to investigate the strange goings-on. Then she took the dogs to meet Lucifer.

It took less than an hour to convince the stallion that she was his friend; it took nearly another hour to coax him to accept the dogs. Born with a gift for handling animals, Pepper was patient and soft-spoken with the horse. And wary. She knew horses—and particularly stallions.

She didn't use carrots or sugar cubes or any other enticement, and she never lifted a hand against the horse. But by the time she'd slid off the fence and onto Lucifer's back for a wild gallop around the pasture, they were friends. The stallion was well trained, responding to the slightest pressure of her knees, and a few moments experimentation bore out her guess that he knew voice commands as well. After that it was downhill all the way.

The sun was well up and warming the frosted ground by the time Pepper climbed up to sit on the top rail of the fence and watch the fruits of her efforts. Lucifer and Fifi were engaged in a playful game of chase at the moment; the Doberman, while cowardly with people, was perfectly cheerful with other animals, and was both quick enough and strong enough to give the stallion a run for his money. Brutus, disdaining lesser pursuits, was down in the hollow investigating the stable.

Pepper enjoyed watching the games, interested as always in personalities—whether or not they were animal or human. She was so caught up in her observation, in fact, that she totally missed the sound of a strange car pulling up in the driveway. But she didn't miss the strange masculine voice.

"Who're you, for God's sake?"

She swung around on the fence, nearly losing her seat, to find herself under scrutiny. Before she could respond, he was speaking again.

"Well, well, well. Don't tell me Thor's been caught at last!"

"I'm working on it," Pepper said involuntarily.

Laughter immediately lit the stranger's golden eyes and filled his deep voice. "Then *you* I've got to meet! D'you mind coming away from that fence for the introductions? Lucifer and I are old enemies."

His name was Cody Nash, and he was a golden man. His thick hair was golden, his tan was golden, his remarkable eyes were golden, and his deep voice held the rough beauty of raw gold.

She pegged him at about Thor's age, although the classical bone structure of his handsome face would probably, she decided, never really show age. Like Thor, he was a tall man, but a couple of inches shorter than Thor and more slender. He was innately charming, friendly, funny, and possessed the kind of looks that had probably broken hearts for years.

Pepper liked him. She liked him immediately and instinctively. Oddly enough, he asked the question Thor hadn't asked, which was, "Pepper what?" She went through the story of how she'd gotten her name, wondering in amusement when it would occur to Thor that he didn't know her entire name. Cody was delighted by the story, returning the favor by explaining that his name had come from an old western novel that his father had been reading in the fathers' waiting room at the hospital.

"So you're a friend of Thor's?" she questioned as they stood a couple of feet back from the fence and watched the canine-equine games.

Cody grimaced slightly. "I think so anyway. We've known each other since we were kids."

Pepper wondered at the answer. Just as she'd picked up constraint in Thor's voice about his job, she heard the same thing now in Cody's voice. And her mind came up with a possible answer. "Did you two have a falling out over some girl?" she asked lightly.

"If only it were that simple," Cody said wryly.

She looked at him inquiringly, not wanting to ask outright but intensely curious.

Abruptly Cody asked, "Were you serious about—uh—working on Thor?"

"Very much so," she answered steadily.

He looked at her for a moment, then nodded slightly. "I see you are. Well, then." His gaze went out over the pasture . . . or over the years. "We were friends all through school, through college, and just normally competitive over girls—the way all boys are after a certain age. But there was nothing serious for either of us. That was in Texas."

Pepper looked at him, startled, but didn't interrupt.

"After school we drifted apart a little—and that's normal too. We had different jobs, and both of us traveled. Thor settled down up here after his parents died; I was still traveling quite a bit. Whenever I wound up in the Northeast, I dropped in. We still tried to take each other's money at poker and kept up a running chess game for a while.

"But gradually—" Cody broke off and shook his head slightly. "I don't know. Something changed. Thor . . . Thor wasn't the same. Oh, not unfriendly. Just not overly friendly. Let's just say that I wasn't encouraged to keep dropping in on the spur of the moment."

"But here you are," she murmured.

"Here I am." He laughed a little ruefully. "I turn up every few months whether he likes it or not. I don't always catch him at home, but when I do, I usually stay a day or two."

"Why?" she asked bluntly. "I mean, why d'you keep coming around?"

"He's my friend," Cody said simply.

Pepper stared at the serious man beside her for a moment, then looked out over the pasture. She thought that she might be seeing a different Thor today because Cody was here, and she wasn't sure she wanted that.

Certainly she wanted to know Thor in all his moods, but she was afraid that this one was going to disturb her. Things were bound to be strained between her and Thor after last night, and any additional tension was not going to be fun to deal with.

She wasn't able to give another thought to this problem, though. A tiny brown fury suddenly erupted from beneath the bottom rail of the fence, yapping hysterically and launching himself with murderous intent at Cody's ankle.

"Hell's bells!" Cody stared down at his would-be assassin in lively astonishment. "I'm being savaged!"

From behind them a laconic voice said, "Welcome to the menagerie."

Six

The next few minutes were rather full. While Pepper was rescuing Cody from the clutches of the wantonly protective Brutus, Thor, with a totally deadpan expression, explained Brutus's attack training. By the time Pepper had the growling Chihuahua tucked under her arm and while Cody's bemusement was holding him silent, Thor suddenly took note of the other pet cavorting in the pasture with his killer horse.

"What the hell—?"

"It's all right, Thor; I introduced them."

"You what?"

"Introduced them. They're friends now. I didn't want you to have to keep shutting Lucifer in his stall whenever the dogs were outside, so I—"

"Pepper, that horse is a killer! And he hates dogs."

"He doesn't hate our dogs." Pepper took no

notice of the pronoun, and Thor was too upset to notice, but Cody filed it away in his bemused brain. "Stop fussing, Thor. He's a very well-trained horse. Did you train him? The slightest knee-pressure, and—"

"*You rode that horse?*"

"Well, just once around the pasture, but—"

Thor erupted. He swore violently and at great length, mostly in English but with a smattering of Spanish and what sounded like a few words of Arabic. He poured wrath over Pepper by the bucketful, and for ten solid minutes never once repeated himself.

Cody stood with arms folded across his chest, staring at his friend with an expression somewhere between the mildly astonished and the totally stunned, from which Pepper gathered that Thor didn't often explode.

As for herself, Pepper stood listening politely and waited for him to run down. Having heard quite a few explosions in her time, she was well aware that this one had been detonated by anxiety along the lines of You-could-have-gotten-your-stupid-self-killed-you-idiot-and-why-the-hell-didn't-you-have-more-sense?

She was enjoying it thoroughly.

He finally began repeating himself, and Pepper decided that it was time to interrupt. "Jean's here," she said, cheerfully breaking in on a sentence calculated to make her hair stand on end. "I think I'll go help her with breakfast. You'd better feed Lucifer, Thor, if you can pry him away from Fifi. And send the mutt on up to the house so I can feed her. See you." She strolled off toward the house, still carrying Brutus tucked underneath an arm.

Venturing to intrude on Thor's fulminating silence, Cody said mildly, "She's quite a lady, Thor. Where'd you find her?"

Thor dragged his glare away from Pepper's retreating back and fastened it onto Cody's hapless person. "Oh, shut up!" he snapped violently, and stalked away to feed his killer horse.

After the emotional tumult of the day before and his sleepless night, Thor was in no mood to deal with the sudden arrival of Cody. And Pepper's recklessness where Lucifer was concerned hadn't helped. And, though she'd been her normal cheerful and absurd self, he'd taken note of the red-rimmed eyes; the image of her crying herself to sleep last night haunted him.

By the time he and a prudently silent Cody entered the house, Thor had himself under nominal control. The slightest spark, and he knew he'd go up like a rocket though.

Ordered cavalierly into the dining room by Mrs. Small, he found that his and Cody's breakfast consisted of omelets.

"Spanish. Pepper's recipe. Authentic," Mrs. Small told him, plunking the plates down on the table.

"Well, where is she?" Thor asked irritably.

The housekeeper looked down her nose at him. "In the kitchen. She's—"

"Tell her she can damn well get her butt in here and eat with us," Thor ordered. "No more skipping meals."

Mrs. Small lifted an eyebrow at him, then returned to the kitchen.

A moment later Pepper came in bearing a plate.

"Omelets," she announced mildly, "are cooked one at a time. I was fixing mine." Sitting down at Thor's left hand, she looked across the table at Cody and added solemnly, "He's so masterful."

Cody's laugh changed itself to a hasty little cough, and he bent his attention to his omelet. Thor, feeling a bit like a fool, glared down at his food and dug in.

"My Spanish omelets are very spicy, you know," Pepper said conversationally just as both men reached hastily for water glasses. "Cayenne pepper." She ate calmly without recourse to her water.

"You don't say?" Cody wheezed.

"Unusual," Thor managed.

"I like food with body. We're having shrimp curry tonight, by the way. I hope you gentlemen'll like it."

Mrs. Small passed through the dining room just then with a dustcloth. "India," she contributed in a satisfied voice. "Authentic."

Thor felt a sudden inclination to go off into a corner and have a quiet nervous breakdown. But he couldn't stay angry. He wanted to burst out laughing at the bemusement on Cody's face, even while realizing wryly that he himself was probably wearing much the same expression. Damn the woman—why'd she keep on knocking him off-balance like this? He felt like a yo-yo.

"You've been to India?" Cody was asking with keen interest in his tone of voice.

"Delhi," Pepper answered easily. "Beautiful place. Thor, I called Mom yesterday and gave her this number, so I'll probably start getting calls. Don't be surprised if my friends sound like nuts."

"That wouldn't surprise me," Thor said definitely.

Laughter lit her eyes. "I'm sure. Oh, and I've got

at least a dozen clients coming today, so the place is apt to be noisy; they're all talkers, I'm afraid."

"Clients?" Cody looked bewildered.

"Dogs." Pepper smiled at him. "I'm grooming dogs for a friend of mine, and Thor's letting me use his mudroom."

"Oh." Fascination was beginning to grip Cody's mobile features. "You—uh—groom dogs?"

"She does everything," Thor told him ruefully. "And she's good at games. Don't play poker with her."

"She's that good?" Cody asked as if she weren't present.

"She cheats. Cardsharp."

"Imagine that." The blond man turned his thoughtful eyes back to Pepper. "An expert at sleight of hand, are you?"

Smiling, Pepper rose with her empty plate and started around the back of Thor's chair. Pausing for only a moment, she demonstrated marvelous legerdemain by neatly removing a coin from Thor's ear. Still smiling gently, she tossed the coin to Cody and went out to the kitchen.

Cody stared down at the quarter while Thor cautiously felt his ear.

"Thor," Cody said in a contemplative voice, continuing to gaze at the coin, "where *did* you find her?"

"I answered an ad in the paper," Thor said carefully, and then broke apart.

However he'd responded to Cody during the past years, Thor was clearly unable to be "not overly friendly" with Papper's strongly felt presence raining absurdity on all of them. From breakfast the day was duly launched along those lines, and it would have taken a stronger man than Thor to resist laughter.

It began with the deluge of the "clients," all arriving within ten minutes of one another. Without Tim, her helper, Pepper had something of a struggle on her hands trying to get all the dogs into their wire kennels. Such a time, in fact, that one toy poddle and two Pekingese escaped her and invaded the den, where Thor and Cody were playing a game of chess.

"Grab 'em!" Pepper yelped from the doorway. "Chico eats pillows and Malfi's Rising Star *refuses* to be housebroken!"

Neither Thor nor Cody wasted time in wanting to know which dog was which; both lunged for the invaders. Thor scooped up a golden Peke that already had its teeth into a pillow on the couch, while Cody dexterously snared the tiny black poodle that was sniffing thoughtfully at the leg of the coffee table. Pepper cornered the remaining brown Peke near the fireplace.

"What the hell?" Thor managed, firmly removing the pillow from sharp little teeth.

"Sorry," Pepper gasped, trying not to laugh. "They got away from me."

"Obviously."

"Which is which?" Cody asked, subjecting his poddle to a critical stare. "Have I got Malfi's— What was it?"

"Malfi's Rising Star. Yes, you've got him. Thor's got Chico, and I've got Duchess. Whose move is it?"

Thor glanced automatically down at the chessboard. "Cody's."

"Move the bishop," Pepper told Cody. She tucked Duchess under one arm, Chico under another, and somehow managed to retrieve Malfi's Rising Star from Cody before leaving the room.

Cody stared down at the board for a moment, then decisively moved the bishop. He grinned at Thor. "She's right. Mate in three moves."

Thor made a rude noise and sat back down to try and win back the ground Pepper had cost him.

Their game was relatively undisturbed for a while, Thor getting up only once to check on the sound of the motorcycle that heralded Tim's arrival. Then the phone began to ring. Thor answered it since Mrs. Small was busy in the kitchen.

"Hello?"

"Hello there. Is Pepper around, or have you buried her?"

Thor took the receiver away from his ear to stare at it for a moment, then replied to the cheerful masculine voice. "She's here. Hold on a minute."

"Sure."

Thor yelled to Mrs. Small, who passed the message on to Pepper. She came in the den with a harassed expression, drying her hands on a towel.

"I wonder why Noah didn't leave poodles off his ark?" she murmured despairingly to the two men, then picked up the phone before either could attempt an answer. "Hello? Oh, hi! No, I was just bathing Malfi's Rising Star. Don't laugh; he's a prize-winning poodle. Who? Oh, that was just Thor."

Thor, listening intently, lost his knight in an absent move and sent a glare toward Pepper. She smiled gently at him and went on with the conversation.

"Yes, Yes. What? No, that was Istanbul. Of course, I'm sure! Well, I bought the thing, didn't I?

It was Istanbul. No, the sari came from India. What *is* this anyway? You taking inventory? Oh. Oh, I see. Well, tell Marsha that saris come from India and sarongs from the Orient. Yes. Okay, fine. See you." She hung up the phone, smiled faintly at the two men staring at her, and headed back for the mudroom.

"Istanbul?" Cody asked plaintively.

Thor sighed. "Don't look at me. I haven't figured her out yet."

They went back to the game. But they were destined to listen in on three more conversations, Pepper's end of them, anyway. None of them made sense. The callers were male, male, and female respectively, which was all that Thor could attest to. Unless, of course, he could offer his opinion that all three callers were holding onto their sanity by the skin of their teeth.

But Pepper's end of the conversations was intriguing.

"You did what? That wasn't very smart. Oh, really? Well, why did you listen to him? That's ridiculous! Just because she's from Hong Kong— I hope you decked him. Oh, good! Both eyes? Nice going, hero. Raw steak. Really, it works very well. Of course, I'm sure. Oh, does she? Well, some of those ancient remedies are terrific, you know. No. No, I'll probably be down that way in a few weeks. Sure. Hey—call Cal and tell him; he'll get a kick out of it. Okay. Bye."

"No, I'm grooming Kristen's dogs. England. An English breeder. If you keep laughing like that, you'll hurt yourself. Of course, she doesn't realize—what a ridiculous question! Him either. A dog show. Me? In London. A friend of a friend, you know. Who? That was Thor. Don't bother; I'm taking all the best god-of-thunder jokes. I'm working on it. No, very nice. Look, if you called just to exercise your giggle box— What? Men have giggle boxes, idiot. And yours is upside down. Funny, that's funny. Right. Okay, you— What? Oh. Belladonna. Yes, the berries are poisonous. You need the whole plant? Let's see . . . Hemlock then. Seeds, leaves, and roots. Of course, I'm sure. Okay, bye."

"Hemlock?" Cody murmured uneasily. "D'you suppose he wants to poison somebody?"

"Beats the hell out of me," Thor said.

Cody reflected for a moment. "An ad in the paper, you said."

"Uh-huh."

"Oh, hi! When did you get back? Really? Did he give you that cute little chalet halfway up? Good. Wasn't the view terrific? Well, I'd think you could have stuck your heads out at least once! What's the use of being in the Alps unless you— Did you? That's something, anyway! Paris, huh? Who? Oh, did he? A running chess game. No, for six months while I was on the Left Bank. Didn't he tell you? No, they raided that club; that's how we met. I wasn't doing anything, I was just there. Overnight. Everybody else slept and we played chess. Did he say that? Liar! He only arrested me so I'd give him a game; nobody else was up to his weight. No, he never put it on the records. Did you tell him that?

Well, I'll give him a call sometime. Sure. Don't mention it. Give him my love, okay? Bye."

By then Thor's game was in shreds. "Arrested," he muttered, staring across the board at Cody. "Good Lord!"

"Sounded harmless," Cody ventured cautiously.

"She's probably wanted for murder somewhere."

"You think so?"

"Hell, I— Oh, never mind. I concede the game, dammit. Let's try poker."

"You're the host."

Lunch turned out to be run-of-the-mill steak and salad, which prompted Thor to ask Mrs. Small sardonically if she'd run out of "Pepper's Authentic Recipes," a question she didn't deign to answer. Pepper turned up for the meal looking even more harassed, and accused Thor of trying to drive her to an early grave.

"I think you've got that backward," he told her.

"No, I haven't. You let Brutus and Fifi out hours ago, and they found something to roll in that smells terrible. Tim's gone home for lunch, and the pets have to stay out in the mudroom until I can wash them."

"So?" Thor was unsympathetic.

Pepper glared at him. "So Brutus is taunting Malfi's Rising Star through the wire and Fifi thinks she's being punished! She's almost hysterical!"

Cody choked on his baked potato, and Thor pounded him on the back with more force than necessary.

"Quit it!" Cody managed, eyes watering.

Pepper took her seat in something of a huff, but

her normally sunny temper rapidly reasserted itself and she became cheerful again. "Oh, well. At least most of the clients are done. There's just Sunnydale to do, and none tomorrow. After today I need a break!"

"Don't we all," Thor murmured.

"Funny man. Did you beat him, Cody?"

"The chess game? He conceded."

"Was he a good loser?"

"Not really. He never is."

"Ah. I'd better keep that in mind."

"Really? Why?"

Thor tapped his water glass with his fork. "Hey, guys—guess who's here?"

"The god of thunder, breathing fire," Pepper murmured.

"Striking sparks with his magic hammer," Cody contributed solemnly.

"Why didn't my parents name me George?" Thor asked the ceiling.

Pepper subjected him to a critical scrutiny. "You don't look like a George. You look like a Thor."

"Thanks."

"Don't mention it."

"Do I look like a Cody?" Cody asked politely.

Pepper gave him the same critical appraisal. "Yes."

"Brief and to the point," Cody noted dryly.

"You asked."

"She's honest," Thor told his friend.

"A woman in a million, in fact." Cody was approving.

Thor winced. "Well, there's honesty . . . and then there's *honesty*."

Trying to hide her amusement, Pepper looked at

him gravely. "Would you like me to lie a little? I can, you know. With the best of them."

Thor looked as though there were quite a few things he could have said to that had Cody not been present. Instead, he said wryly, "Of course you can; you're a woman."

It was Pepper's turn to wince. "Damn, could I get you with that one! I hate blanket statements." Quite deliberately she added, "Besides, if you haven't learned by now not to stick any kind of label on me, then there is something badly wrong with your faculties."

Thor sipped iced tea and stared at her over the rim of her glass, refusing to be drawn. It was Cody who had a remark to follow hers.

"It occurs to me," he said consideringly as he gazed at Pepper, "that for all your little-girl voice and lack of inches, you are a formidable lady."

Pepper looked at him, totally deadpan. "Better men than you have learned that—to their cost," she said, and lifted an eyebrow at him.

After a moment, Cody turned a mournful stare on Thor. "My friend, you are down for the count."

Thor choked slightly, taken by surprise since he was unaware that Pepper had blurted out her true intentions to Cody after barely laying eyes on him. Before he could respond, Pepper did.

"The count is nine," she murmured, demonstrating a knowledge of boxing terminology. Rising with her cleared plate, she added a *tsk-tsk* sound and said, "Kayoed—and at his age too." She went away to the kitchen.

"An ad in a newspaper," Cody said slowly.

Thor could only nod.

"Classified?"

"Uh-huh."

"Did she come with Green Stamps?"

"If you want a bed to sleep in tonight," Thor said threateningly, "shut up."

"Uh . . . yes."

The rest of the day went smoothly—compared to the morning. Pepper finished the grooming of the last of her clients and left Tim to watch over them until their proud owners picked them up. She got Brutus and Fifi cleaned up, then went and took a shower herself.

When she came back downstairs, she found Thor sharing the den with two disgruntled pets. Brutus was sulking after the indignity of a bath, and Fifi was lying as close as possible to Thor's chair and looking nervous. Thor was absently shuffling a deck of playing cards.

"Where's Cody?" Pepper asked as she came into the room.

"Pestering Mrs. Small." Thor looked at her, eyes hooded. "It's a favorite pastime of his."

Pepper laughed. "It figures." She went over to sit on the couch, pushing Brutus to one side and ignoring his irritated grumble.

"I'm sorry about last night," Thor said suddenly.

Determined to keep it light, Pepper said, "Sorry you left so abruptly? Or sorry that it happened at all?" Belatedly she realized that this was their first moment alone together since last night.

He smiled a little. "Sorry I left so abruptly."

She shrugged. "Well, I did sort of hit you over the head, didn't I? I seem to have lost all ability to be . . . subtle."

Thor stared at her for a long moment. When he spoke, his words came slowly, consideringly, but his voice was raw around the edges. "Do you know . . . I've been through more emotions in the past twenty-four hours than I have in years. From amusement to absolute fury. And through it all— through it all, I've wanted you more and more with every second that passed."

Pepper swallowed hard. "You don't like it."

"No."

"I'm sorry."

"Are you? What about the chase?"

She glanced down as Brutus gave up his sulks and climbed into her lap. Absently she petted him. "I don't know, Thor. I just know that I'm sorry you feel that way. I feel as if . . . as if I've known you for a long time. I feel as if you should be my friend. But whenever I look at you and think *friend*, then I see *lover*. As if you can't be one or the other without being both. I've never looked at a man that way. I don't know quite how to deal with that."

Thor waited until she met his steady gaze, then said with odd gentleness, "Brave talk aside?"

Pepper smiled, recalling her arrogant remarks about chasing all the way to hell and knockout punches. "Brave talk aside. When you're small, you learn to talk big—or get run over. You also learn determination." Her violet eyes were direct. "I may lose this time, Thor, but I'll know why."

He nodded slowly, understanding what she was telling him. Win or lose, Pepper meant to find out why he avoided commitment. He could hardly blame her for that. Truth to tell, he wanted her to know. But he wasn't yet ready to tell her. And that bothered him, because he understood why. In the past he'd never hesitated to let a woman know why he avoided ties. Now he was hesitating.

Not because Pepper mattered too little . . . but because she mattered too much.

"Truce?" She was smiling at him. "I think we need a little breathing time, Thor."

"Things have been happening a bit rapidly," he agreed in a regretful tone.

"You can say that again!" She laughed unsteadily.

"Truce then. We'll slow the carousel before we both fall off."

Pepper grinned. "You know—between imagery, analogies, and metaphors, I think we've invented our own language!"

"I've always wanted to do that."

"Fun, isn't it?"

"Hello, all," Cody said, coming into the room.

"It's the one-eyed jack," Thor told Pepper.

"Better than a suicide king," she said solemnly.

"Not if jacks are wild."

"Are they?"

"One-eyed jacks and deuces."

"That sounds reasonable."

Cody cast a bewildered look down at the growling Chihuahua attached to one leg of his jeans, then apparently decided to ignore it since everyone else was. "Not to me, it doesn't. Have I wandered into a verbal poker game?"

"Speaking of which"—Thor briskly shuffled the cards he still held—"why don't we play a few hands? If, that is, Pepper'll push the sleeves of her sweater up and submit to a body search before every hand."

"Oh, that's cute!" she told him dryly.

"It was worth a try."

"Hey, fella, I don't have to cheat to win."

"Let's take her money, Cody."

"I'm game."

"Cut for the deal. Ten of clubs."

"Jack of diamonds," Cody announced. "Go away, Brutus."

"Queen of hearts." Pepper smiled. "I deal."

Thor looked suspicious. "You cut that card every time!"

"Makes you wonder, doesn't it?"

"Push back your sleeves, dammit."

"Will somebody get this savage creature away from my ankle?"

Pepper didn't win every hand. Just most of them.

With a truce declared and scrupulously honored by both sides, an odd sort of harmony settled into their relationship. It was aided during the first couple of days by Cody, who was, whether he was aware of it or not, a buffer who allowed them to find the distance they needed.

Since Pepper was free of her grooming duties on Wednesday, all three spent the day just enjoying themselves. They played chess and cards and charades indoors. They raked leaves outside because of the windy night before, finishing with the inevitable leaf-fight. All three were energetic, athletic, and competitive, which meant that they were exhausted by the end of the day.

Mrs. Small continued to lay before them various culinary examples of Pepper's travels, leaving palates in a state of perpetual shock. Brutus attacked Cody about every three hours—apparently on principle.

Cody left early Thursday morning, his only comment on the relationship being a private one to Pepper just before he went.

"Stick around, huh? You've been good for him."

His words were good for Pepper. He knew Thor better than she did, after all, and if he approved . . . well, it shored up her flagging confidence. In the meantime, however, the truce went on.

Pepper taught Thor to deal crooked hands at poker, argued furiously with him over which team was best on televised football games, and soundly defeated him at chess for four solid days before he discovered that he was able to psych her out by carrying on a ridiculous conversation all the while.

His favorite method was to conduct a guessing game as to how exactly Pepper had misspent the past years. Although still searching for the pieces to the puzzle, he kept it light and leaned toward the absurd. He might not have learned much about her past that way, but he beat her at chess.

"I know! You're a spy."

"It's your move," she said dryly.

"A double agent, probably."

"Smile when you say that."

"What's the going rate for spies these days?"

"Cheap. It's a buyer's market."

"No, really? I'd think the other way around."

"There's a waiting list for the spy school," she drawled.

"Maybe I could add my name to the list. Who do I see about that?"

"Your local spy-recruiter, of course."

"Put in a good word for me?"

"Not on your life. Move!" she ordered.

"There."

"Damn."

"Checkmate."

"Arrested in Paris, were you?"

"Eavesdropper."

"Always. Why were you arrested?"

"Jaywalking."

"Funny."

"Great comeback."

"I'll do better next time."

"Do that."

"If not a spy, you were a smuggler."

"Was I?"

"That was a dumb move. I think my guess hit close to home."

"Ridiculous."

"Admit it—I shook you that time."

"Not a chance."

"You're awfully small to be a smuggler."

"I fit into small places."

"True."

"Check."

"Ah. Wasn't a dumb move after all. . . ."

"You know—something's just occurred to me."

"Did anybody ever tell you that you could talk the hind leg off a donkey?"

"Now, that's the pot calling the kettle black with a vengeance!"

"Funny man. What's occurred to your busy brain?"

"I don't know your last name."

"You don't know my first name."

"What? What's Pepper then?"

"A nickname."

"You mean I don't know either of your names?"

"Nope."

"I'm living with a lady whose name I don't know?"

"Looks that way, doesn't it?"

"Well, hell. Tell me then."

"Sorry. You waited too long to ask."

"I'll ask Mrs. Small."

"She won't tell you."

"I'll find your driver's license."

"It's in the van and you promised not to go in there."

"Dammit."

"Checkmate."

"What?"

"I've caught on to your little game now, guy. And two can play it. We'll see who psychs out who."

"Great. That's just great."

"We could arm-wrestle. I'm sure you'd win at that."

"You're a lot of help."

Seven

That first week slipped by and then a second one. Pepper received calls from her friends from time to time, calls to which Thor listened unabashedly and from which he learned absolutely nothing concrete. The clients came and were groomed and left. Meals continued to be exotic. The truce went on.

Since it was always her recipes and never her cooking that Thor sampled, he challenged her assertion of being able to cook on Mrs. Small's next day off. Pepper pulled out all the stops, whipping up culinary masterpieces that would have had the great chefs of Europe crying into their bouillabaisses. By the time a groaning Thor pushed himself away from the table that night, he willingly conceded that Pepper could, indeed, cook.

Thor complimented her solemnly on her "wonderful little feminine talents," which goaded Pepper into sitting up three nights running to knit a scarf for him. She presented the scarf and asked sweetly if he had any buttons that needed sewing on . . . socks to be darned?

He asked if she did windows, and got hit in the middle of his chest with a ball of yarn.

And the truce went on.

But it was wearing thin in spots.

Pepper was finding it increasingly difficult to be relaxed in Thor's company. She caught herself watching him with a fixed intensity, and had to bite her tongue more than once to keep from blurting out in plain words how she felt about him. She tossed and turned at night, restless, her body punishing her for sticking to her rules. When she looked at Thor, a desperate need to touch him haunted her.

There were times when she would have willingly and deliberately broken her rules, times when the need to belong to him—however briefly—tortured her. And it wasn't the fear of defeat that kept her from breaking her rules, but a new fear of what would happen afterward if she did. She had discovered that love was not a gentle emotion, and that it was not something she'd be able to put behind her without regret. When—if—she had to leave him, it would be bad. Very bad.

Toward the end of that second week their relationship altered in a far from subtle manner. And it was all Thor's fault. Whether he realized that she was wavering or was just following his own instincts, he'd apparently decided that a truce didn't necessarily mean a laying down of *all* arms.

Along those lines he employed the one weapon Pepper couldn't fight with her wits or her ability as a gameswoman, the one weapon that would break her in the end if anything did.

He began to act like a lover.

It was small things at first. A light touch. A playful slap on the fanny. A hand toying absently with her hair whenever he was near enough—and he almost always was. A kiss on her nose.

Then the light touches began to linger, and the kisses fell on her lips more often than on her nose. He watched her like a cat at a mousehole, and his smile made her increasingly nervous. He smiled at her, she thought, as though she were chocolate cake . . . and it were time for dessert.

"You're staring at me."

"Of course."

"Why?"

"I like staring at you."

"It makes me nervous."

"Good."

"What d'you mean, *good*?"

"I want to make you nervous."

"Again, *why*?"

"I believe I told you once that these days a man needs every edge he can find or steal."

"Get Brutus off the coffee table, will you?"

"Changing the subject?"

"Why don't we roast marshmallows?"

"You're cute when you're nervous."

For the first time in her life Pepper had the uneasy suspicion that she'd painted herself into a corner. And though she was not a woman given to panic, Pepper was halfway there. Falling back on her wits, she decided finally to show Thor a few more puzzle pieces in the hope that it would distract him from his own strategy. And since she always felt uncomfortable talking about herself, the tactic called for a couple of her nutty friends.

It didn't take her long to choose between them.

After casually asking Thor if he minded, she called Cal and Marsha Brenner and invited them to visit. They were more than willing to drive up from New Hampshire, mostly intrigued by Pepper's current residence and what she was doing there. Of all her friends they were the friendliest and most talkative, and she had no doubt that either of them would talk about her to Thor if he asked.

Pepper wasn't quite sure what she hoped to accomplish by the tactic. She told herself sternly that Thor needed to know more about her, but a wry little voice in her head said that she just wanted a buffer for a day.

She ignored the voice.

The Brenners arrived late on Sunday morning, driving their beat-up Mustang and radiating good humor. Introductions were performed, and all four stood for a while near the garage and talked casually.

Cal Brenner was average in height and build, with a lazy voice and rather penetrating blue eyes. His wife, Marsha, was several inches taller than Pepper and had copper-colored hair and green eyes. She was quite strikingly beautiful. Her voice was deep and rich and seemed constantly full of laughter.

The conversation was innocent and casual at first, consisting mainly of descriptions of the scenery along the newcomers' route from New Hampshire. But it took an abrupt and bewildering turn within moments of their arrival.

Marsha, who had been watching Pepper narrowly for some time, suddenly emitted what sounded like a gurgle of suppressed laughter.

Then the laughter was gone as though it had never existed, and she was leaning forward slightly. Placing her hands on Thor's shoulders, she gazed up into his startled eyes with an expression of heartrending pity.

"Oh, you poor man!" she said intensely.

Thor stared at her blankly for a moment, then looked over at Pepper. She was leaning against her RV and gazing pensively up at the clear blue sky. Helplessly Thor turned his pleading eyes to Cal.

The other man stood with arms folded across his chest. Obviously taking pity on his host's bewilderment, he said gravely, "You'll have to excuse my wife. She's always wanted to be an actress; sometimes she gets carried away."

"I can't bear it!" Marsha wailed suddenly, turning away from Thor to prop an arm against the garage and rest her forehead on it. "I can't bear it—another free spirit shackled!"

A bit desperately Thor asked Cal, "What part's she playing now, Lady Macbeth?"

Marsha momentarily dispensed with the histrionics to tell him reprovingly, "You don't know your Shakespeare."

Thor shook his head slightly to clear the mists, then glanced at Pepper again. She was solemnly studying her fingernails and whistling softly between her teeth. He looked back at Cal. "D'you mind throwing a little light on the situation?"

Cal looked thoughtful. "Well, as I said, Marsha wanted to be an actress. But before Broadway or Hollywood could discover her, Pepper did. And Pepper gave her to me."

"I beg your pardon?" Thor asked, thoroughly baffled now.

"Threw her at me actually. Of course, she was

throwing me at Marsha at the same time. A veritable clash of the Titans. It took nearly a year, and some fancy footwork, but our Pepper got the knot tied in the end."

"I'm still in the dark," Thor protested.

"She's a matchmaker, you know. Renowned worldwide. In fact, I personally know of one sheikh who's taken up monogamy because of Pepper. Shocked his entire kingdom. An Arab sheikh without a harem? Boggles the mind."

While Thor was still swimming through the seas of bewilderment, Marsha lifted her head and directed a stern glance at Pepper. "Does he go to his fate blindly unsuspecting?" she asked.

"Oh, no." Pepper smiled gently at Thor. "He's been warned."

Marsha abandoned her role to turn around and lean back against the garage. "Boy, am I going to enjoy this! We ought to sell tickets; the whole gang would turn up for ringside seats."

"Somebody tell me what you're talking about," Thor requested, but he already knew.

Marsha smiled at him, devilment dancing in her green eyes. "Well, since my husband has been at great pains not to put the matter bluntly, I'd be glad to. You see, we have a slight advantage over you; we've known Pepper longer. So we know that once Pepper gets her hook into a fish, *he's landed*."

Thor looked from her laughing face to Cal's bland one, and then at Pepper. She was still smiling at him. "I see. I'm the fish."

Marsha nodded. "That's it. And what makes it so enjoyable for us is that Pepper has never hooked a fish for herself before. Her footwork this time should be well worth watching."

Dispassionately Cal said, "She doesn't look it, and God knows she doesn't sound it, but Pepper is the most dangerous woman I've ever met. Heart of gold, mind you, but ruthless as hell."

Thor stared at Pepper. "I think I should have paid more attention to that warning."

"Too late now," she murmured, and came forward to link her arm with Marsha's. "Come along, friend. Let's go and see what we can dig up in Mrs. Small's kitchen."

"Isn't it Thor's kitchen?" Marsha asked interestedly.

"No. His home and her castle."

"Ah. Lead the way."

They strolled off.

Thor stared after them for a moment, then looked at Cal. "And I thought Pepper was the only nut. I think there's a treeful of them. No offense."

"None taken." Cal grinned. "Welcome to the tree."

"It isn't an accomplished fact, you know," Thor reminded him, wondering if he should be worried that he felt more amused than trapped.

"Isn't it?"

Thor decided to avoid the polite question. He leaned back against the Corvette. "So tell me—since you've known her longer—about Pepper. One short paragraph, if possible." Thor was determined to find out everything he could from these friends of Pepper's, no matter how underhanded it might be to pump them.

"Can't be done, I'm afraid." Cal smiled slightly. "Unless you'd like the definition we've accepted for years."

"Which is?"

"That Pepper is an enigma wrapped up in a puzzle within a mystery—followed by a question mark."

"How long have you known her?"

"Ten years. She was three years behind me at Stanford."

"Stanford?" Thor blinked. "Well, well. She didn't mention that."

"Uh. Phi Beta Kappa. Summa cum laude."

Thor's eyebrows rose. "Didn't mention that either. What else hasn't she mentioned to me?"

"Probably most of her life." Cal shrugged slightly. "She's an odd one, our Pepper. Doesn't talk much about herself. What she does say is just mentioned in passing—people she's met, or places she's been. She doesn't try to be mysterious, she just thinks that other people are more interesting than she is. Our gang, the crowd formed during college days, has pieced together some things. But not much."

"For instance?"

Cal looked at him directly. "Does it matter?"

Thor met the steady gaze and realized that Pepper had loyal friends. And that this one, at least, wasn't going to reveal anything about his friend to a man with only a casual interest. "It matters," he told Cal, and knew then that it *did* matter. Dammit, it was no longer a game—if it ever had been. And, whatever it was, he was no longer certain that he wanted to win.

Without pushing or questioning, Cal simply nodded. "She was born and raised in Texas, but since she hasn't been back there in more than ten years, we assume she doesn't consider it home."

Thor was a little startled by this first bit of information. Texas? An odd coincidence. She certainly didn't possess a Texas drawl; in fact, her breathless little-girl voice had no accent of any kind. A result of her years of travel, perhaps? Before he could consider the matter further, Cal was going on.

"Started at Stanford at seventeen. Her father died about then, and apparently he left her an inheritance and told her to see the world. She always took off during vacations and holidays, bringing back gifts for the rest of us from all over the world. She never talked about her trips except for bits and pieces mentioned in passing. We learned not to ask questions about where she'd been. Pepper has a marvelous ability to head you off until you find yourself talking about something entirely different.

"Since college . . . I know a little, and can guess a little. She travels regularly now, out of the country more often than she's in it. She leaves the RV and the pets with her mother, who lives here in the East. If we want to contact Pepper, we call her mother, who usually has a number where we can reach her. And—well, she just goes."

"Alone?"

"As far as I know. She sometimes comes back with company though. She found Marsha stranded in London and brought her back. And several other members of our gang were discovered by her in various improbable parts of the globe. And I do mean improbable. Mae—who's now married to Brian, who was one of the founding members of our group—is from Hong Kong. Pepper brought her over to visit, she said, and had them married before the visa expired.

"Then there's Heather from Scotland and now married to Tom. And Jean-Paul, who came, of course, from France—"

"Jean-Paul?" Thor queried with all the American male's distrust of Frenchmen.

Reading the tone correctly, Cal chuckled. "You should meet him. He's an artist—a damn good one, as a matter of fact—and absolutely adores his 'Angelique.' He and Angela were married last year. Another of Pepper's matches."

"She sounds like the United Nations," Thor said in astonishment.

Cal shrugged. "What can I tell you? She likes her friends to be happy."

"And are they?"

"Oh, yes. Pepper has an uncanny knack for matching people with the right partners. Not a divorce or separation in the lot, and for some of us it's been a few years. She's batting a thousand."

Thor was silent for a moment, trying to fit pieces together and come up with a complete picture of a woman who was still largely unknown to him. Finally he shook his head. "The more I hear, the less I know."

Cal looked at him with a certain amount of sympathy. "Yeah, I know the feeling. There isn't much more I can tell you. She usually manages to drop in on us whenever she comes back to the States. We don't ask questions; she doesn't offer answers. In spite of her sometimes talkative ways, Pepper doesn't let a lot of herself out into the open."

Suddenly, and for the first time in his life, Thor felt a feeling so strong and so savage that he had to look away from the other man. And in that moment he was literally afraid to move or speak, because he didn't think he could be responsible for his actions or words. It had been building within him for long moments now, and he'd known it without recognizing the sensation.

Intellect struggled with two million years of instinct, and Thor wasn't sure which would win.

His scant knowledge of both Pepper and Cal told him rationally that theirs was a friendship and nothing more, but instinct as old as the cave fiercely resented the ten years they had known each other. Resented those years with an irrational and bedeviled jealousy.

Intellect won the struggle, but it left Thor feeling shaken and oddly out of his depth. He could neither forget nor ignore the jealousy, but he was at least able to shut it away in a small room in his mind where it chased itself in vicious circles. Not a solution, of course, but that way it wouldn't savagely attack Pepper's friend.

Thor dragged his thoughts from that subject and realized Cal was watching him curiously. But before the other man could question what, Thor surmized, had probably been a peculiar expression, Marsha stuck her head out the front door and called to them.

"Hey, you two! Pepper's found some stuff and she's going to make shish kebab. Think you heroes can start a fire in that monstrosity of a barbecue out back?"

"We'll do our best," Cal called back dryly. As she disappeared back inside the house, he looked at Thor. "We have our orders."

"Uh-huh." Locked room or no, Thor badly needed an outlet for the various types of frustration building within him, and that very emotion was reflected in his voice when he went on irritably. "Shish kebab. Dammit, is there anything that woman *can't* do? She cooks, sews, knits, and drives that monster RV of hers as if she'd driven a semi for years. She's got my 'vicious' stallion eating out of her hand. She plays the piano beautifully. She's a cardsharp. She knows enough about football to call the plays at a Super Bowl game, and enough about chess to be a grand master at the game—"

"She is," Cal murmured helpfully. "Bona fide. Won an international competition in Bonn a couple of years ago. Impressed the hell out of the judges since she was so young. Of course, an unkind soul could point out that she probably rattled her opponent by looking dumb and sweet, but—"

"But"—Thor interrupted with a goaded glare—"she was probably *born* a grand master." He released a sigh compounded of a groan and a growl. "She's not real. I don't believe in perfection, particularly in people. She has to have a fault somewhere—she has to!"

Cal frowned thoughtfully for a moment, then lifted a triumphant finger. "She's stubborn!"

Glaring at him, Thor muttered, "You're a lot of help."

"Sorry." Cal was smiling.

"Hell. Let's go get that fire started."

"Cheer up," Cal advised gravely. "It could be worse, you know."

"Yeah? How, for God's sake?"

"She might not have warned you at all. At least you don't go to your fate—uh—blindly unsuspecting."

"Dammit."

"Looked like they were having quite an interesting little chat," Marsha announced to her friend, coming back into the kitchen.

Pepper was chopping meat on the cutting board,

and glanced up with a slight smile. "I'm not at all surprised, considering that little scene you and Cal were playing."

"Who was playing?" Marsha was cheerfully unrepentant. "Besides, it was a scream. Did you see Thor's face?"

"I saw it." Pepper laughed in spite of herself. "You ought to be ashamed of yourself, and so should I; the man must think I'm after his scalp by now."

"Well, aren't you?" Marsha asked with a grin.

"Not with a knife."

"So he keeps his hair but loses his freedom, huh?"

Pepper bent her head over her task and was silent for a long moment. Then, with unusual asperity, she burst out, "Is that what I'm doing—depriving him of his freedom?"

Startled, Marsha looked over from the sink, where she'd been washing tomatoes and onions. She turned off the water and slowly dried her hands on a paper towel, staring at her friend. "Hey, I was kidding, Pepper."

Pepper shook her head slightly. "I know. But the question's still there, Marsha. If I win . . . does he lose?"

"Is it a game?" her friend asked soberly.

"Maybe he thinks it is. Maybe he thinks that one of us can lose, and that we'll both end up with a nice little memory."

"But . . . ?"

"But . . ." Pepper sighed softly. "I don't think it'll end that way. In the beginning I thought that if I won, we'd both win. You know, in love and loving it." She laughed suddenly, harshly. "Vain of me, I realize. But I've always believed that happiness meant love and sharing."

"And now you don't believe that?"

"I don't know. It's . . . it's not a gentle emotion, is it? I never knew that." She smiled crookedly at her friend. "Now I understand what kind of wringer I put the rest of you through. Would an apology on bended knees make amends?"

Marsha smiled in return. "No need. People rarely fall in love totally against their will, Pepper; not one of us regrets your matchmaking."

"I'm glad," Pepper said simply.

"You won't get away with changing the subject this time," Marsha said conversationally. "For once, you're going to bend my ear—even if I have to badger you to do it. So. What makes you think Thor would lose if you win?"

"He doesn't want permanent ties."

"So?"

"So who am I to think he'd be happier tied to me?"

"Bad phrase, that," Marsha remarked objectively. " 'Tied to,' I mean. Conjures up images of slavery. We both know that's not what you mean."

Pepper stirred slightly. "I know, I know. But if he values his freedom so much, isn't that what it amounts to?"

"He didn't seem to me to be rabid about his freedom."

"Not rabid. Just determined."

"Whatever."

"It's just that . . . well, what right had I to move in on him? To plunk myself down squarely in the middle of his life as if I belonged here?"

"Do you love him?" Marsha asked bluntly, in the tone of a woman who's sure of the answer.

Pepper stared at her fingers for a long moment, then lifted her gaze to her friend's face. "So much so that I couldn't bear for him to lose anything because of me. I want to add to his life, Marsha, not take away from it. And if that means I'll have to leave him with a nice little memory and a triumphant victory . . . then that's what I'll have to do," Pepper finished softly.

"Have you told him that you love him?" Marsha asked in an equally hushed tone.

"No." Pepper smiled a little. "I won't burden him with something he doesn't want."

Marsha stared at her for a moment, then said caustically, "If you ask me, you're being unnecessarily noble. What makes you so certain it'd be a burden to him?"

"He knows how I feel about love. He knows that if I feel love, I expect something permanent. If I tell him I love him, it'll be a burden to him. He's that kind of man."

"Has it ever occurred to you," Marsha demanded, "that he might just possibly be changing his mind about his desire for 'freedom' even as we speak? Has it occurred to you that perhaps he thought he wanted no ties only because he'd never found the right woman?"

"Yes, it's occurred to me." Pepper laid the knife aside suddenly, aware of the dangers of slicing anything with only half her mind on what she was doing. "It occurs to me constantly." She heard the hard-bitten sound of her own voice and was abruptly grateful that Marsha had stuck firmly to this subject; she needed to talk. "Don't you think I *want* that to be true? Don't you think I lie awake at night and wonder if I'll be able to leave him when the time comes? Dammit, Marsha I want to fling my love at him! I've had to choke back the words a hundred times. I want to . . . to touch him whenever he's near me, and even more when he's away from me. It's hard to breathe when he's there and even worse when he's not."

She laughed unsteadily, a laugh that was a talisman to ward off tears. "I look at you and Cal, and think of the others, and I wonder—my God, did I do this to them? Did I, in my insufferable arrogance, put them through this hell because I thought I knew what was best for them?"

"Pepper—"

"And now this!" Pepper cut off her friend flatly. "Thor. I fall in love for the first time in my life, and I launch a campaign with all the cocky arrogance of a paper-pushing general! And if Thor's freedom is important to him and I win the battle, then he'll be caged. Caged!"

She felt her fingers aching and realized that she was gripping the edge of the counter as though it were a lifeline. With an effort she spoke levelly, almost neutrally. "Have you ever gone to a zoo and watched the cats? They pace. Constantly, endlessly. Do we have the right to do that to them? Animals should never be caged, even if they're given an illusion of freedom. And people should never be caged, even if the bars are formed out of commitments."

"We're all caged," Marsha pointed out quietly. "We're caged by jobs, by a way of life, by people who love us and those whom we love. There are limits to everything, Pepper, boundaries we all observe. You know that as well as I do. And if we had the choice, most of us would choose to keep the boundaries. Because there's something secure in knowing how far you can go."

"But is it fair to place someone else inside our own boundaries?" Pepper looked searchingly at her friend. "That's what bothers me. Thor has his own boundaries; is it fair to demand that he be limited by mine?"

Marsha returned the stare for a moment, then quoted softly, " 'I am the master of my fate; I am the captain of my soul.' Thor strikes me as being both; he's his own man. If he is limited by your boundaries, it'll be because he wants to be—and for no other reason."

Pepper drew a deep, shuddering breath. "I suppose I'm selfish, but I want him inside *my* boundaries."

"You're not selfish. You're in love."

"And I'm afraid of losing." Pepper smiled shakily. "Funny, that's something I haven't been afraid of in years. But I've never gambled like this before; there's never been so much at stake."

Marsha smiled a little. "Follow your instincts, friend. I haven't seen much of him, but I have a feeling that you and your Thor would be deliriously happy together. Go for it."

There was no more teasing that day about Pepper's matchmaking, and no real opportunity for Thor to learn more about her than he already had. But his sudden attack of jealousy had had more of an impact on him than anything Cal had told him about Pepper.

In that moment Thor had realized that it no longer mattered what and who Pepper was or had been. It wasn't important. What mattered was that, like a thorn or a splinter or a virus, she'd somehow managed to burrow beneath his skin. He was no longer *just* fascinated by her.

The other couple left after dinner, steadfastly refusing to stay overnight. They had apparently promised Marsha's mother in Bangor that they'd spend the night with her, and Cal professed himself in dread terror of offending his mother-in-law.

After they'd gone, Pepper sat on the couch absently dealing crooked poker hands on the coffee table and watching from the corner of her eye as Thor paced restlessly. She could feel the tension increasing moment by moment, growing within the room like a living thing. It made her so nervous that she mistakenly dealt a ten into a low straight flush. Swearing softly, she gathered up the cards.

"It isn't a game, is it?" Thor asked suddenly, quietly. He was standing by the front window, staring out. "It was never a game."

Pepper stacked the cards neatly facedown on the coffee table and then sat back, gazing across the room at his broad back. She wasn't surprised by his comment; her little voice inside had been telling her all day that the buffer of her friends had only postponed the inevitable.

Equally quiet, she said, "For me, no; it was never a game. The . . . methods . . . maybe. But I was serious from the start."

"Why me?" he asked, still without turning around.

"Ask me how many angels can dance on the head of a pin," Pepper said wryly. "I'd have a better answer for that."

He turned around, leaning back against the windowframe and looking across at her. She was somehow surprised to see that his expression was calm, his eyes thoughtful. As if his mind were somewhere else, he asked, "How did you get that scar?"

Pepper didn't even consider evasion. Or games. "I was carrying a briefcase full of gems and a man tried to steal them from me," she said calmly.

Eight

Pepper's statement certainly caught Thor's attention. He smiled slowly. "I see. Did you rob a museum?"

She smiled a little. "Not quite. From time to time, I take jobs as a bonded courier. I don't need the money, but I enjoy the . . . the challenge of it. What I've carried most times was something small but valuable that the owner didn't want to entrust to any other method of transport. Stamp collections, old coins, heirlooms."

Making an innocent, empty-handed gesture, she said, "Now I ask you—do I look as if someone would entrust something valuable to me?"

"No," Thor replied dryly.

"The ace up my sleeve." Her smile turned rueful. "I haven't lost anything yet."

Thor nodded toward the scar on her hand. "But someone came close?"

Pepper rubbed a thumb across the mark. "Close only counts in horseshoes."

"What happened?"

"From the beginning?"

"Please."

"A wealthy American collector sold several of his finest pieces to an equally wealthy British collector. About that time there had been more than one jewelry theft on both sides of the Atlantic, and these pieces were very, very valuable. Couriers had been robbed en route; so the collectors decided on a shell game. They sent out several couriers along different routes, all but one empty-handed. I had the gems."

Thor crossed the room slowly to sit down on the couch beside her. "And?" he asked, obviously intrigued.

"There was a leak." Pepper sighed. "Only the two collectors were supposed to know which of us had the jewelry; we found out later that the buyer's valet had decided to go into business for himself. I'll pass up the remark about how hard it is to get good servants these days. Anyway, I made it across the Atlantic and into London in one piece. Unfortunately it was a foggy day in old London Town, which gave the would-be thief excellent cover and loused up my sense of direction.

"I must have run through most of the mews in the city—with him right behind me—before I finally located the buyer's house. And after a conspicuous lack of bobbies for more than two hours, there was one practically on the buyer's doorstep. And . . . well, that's all."

Thor reached over to cover the small, restless hand with its faint scar. "Other than this, did he hurt you?"

"He didn't get the chance!" Pepper grinned. "I'm small, but I'm fast."

Not returning the grin, Thor said slowly, "Dangerous work."

"Not really. Not usually." She shrugged. "I've been a courier for about six years; that jewel thing happened last year, and it was only the second time someone tried to hold me up."

Thor's hand tightened on hers. "What happened the first time?"

Pepper laughed suddenly as the memory flooded her mind. "It was hysterical really. You would have gotten a kick out of it. The poor guy wasn't after the old stamp collection in my case. He was just your average, run-of-the-mill mugger. I was carrying the collection from L.A. to New York, and had a one-night layover in Kansas City.

"I decided to visit some friends there, and I was walking to their apartment when this man yanked me into an alley. There he stood with this rusty pipe, getting ready to brain me. I don't know what made him hesitate, although he said later that it was because he hadn't realized until then that I was so small. Anyway, I had a few seconds to get good and mad, and so I pulled my gun out of my shoulder bag and—"

"Your gun?" Thor seemed equally fascinated and horror-struck.

"Uh-huh. I'm licensed to carry a gun, although I don't do so outside the States of course. It's a forty-five automatic. I've found that nothing makes a potential burglar or mugger more nervous than a very small woman inexpertly waving about a very big gun."

"Are you inexpert?"

"Of course not, but he didn't know that."

"Oh," was all Thor could manage to say.

"Anyway, as soon as he saw the gun he dropped the pipe and started stuttering and shaking. I was cussing him up one side and down the other, and the madder I got, the more he shook—it was really very funny."

"What happened?" Thor asked in the tone of a man who wasn't quite sure he wanted to know.

"I treated him to a hamburger," Pepper said gravely.

"You what?" Thor asked faintly.

"Well, he was hungry. We talked for a while, and then had a hamburger and talked some more. And then I took him with me to my friends' house and he slept on the couch. By the time my plane left the next day, he had a job training horses at a local stable. His name is Henry, and I drop in to see him about once a year. He tells everyone within earshot the story of how we met, and says he has a little Nemesis that makes him keep to the straight and narrow."

"I don't believe it," Thor murmured, staring at her.

"I don't see why not. Henry wasn't a very good mugger, but he turned into a first-rate trainer."

"Matchmaker . . . and mender of lonely hearts." Thor shook his head slightly. "Cal was right. You're an enigma wrapped up in a puzzle surrounded by a mystery—followed by a question mark."

"Cal said that?"

"Yes. After knowing you for ten years, he said that."

Pepper attempted a laugh that didn't quite come off. "I didn't realize I was so complicated."

"But you are." The arm lying along the back of

the couch moved, and his free hand brushed a strand of silver-blond hair away from her face. "You are."

A subdued violence in her tone, she said suddenly, "But I don't want to be! Not to you! Thor, I'm *not* complicated! I'm ordinary!"

"I knew you were prone to understatement the first time I saw that 'van' of yours," he murmured with a tiny smile.

Pepper didn't return the smile. Having finally abandoned the "game," she never looked back. "I'm just a woman, Thor—no more and no less. Oh, sure, I've seen a lot of the world. I've seen things I hope to God I never see again, and I don't suppose ladies carry guns or turn muggers into horse trainers, but that doesn't mean I'm complicated. I laugh and cry and get mad like other women, and— *dammit!*—what's so complicated about that?"

Thor realized that she really wanted to know and he supposed that, from her point of view, she wasn't complicated, but he didn't quite know how to explain her uniqueness. Instead, he smiled suddenly and said, "Tell me your name."

She laughed in spite of herself. "Didn't you ask Cal?"

"I didn't want to admit to ignorance."

Pepper could feel Thor's fingers moving gently at the nape of her neck, and while the little caress sent her nerves jangling, it was also oddly soothing. She smiled at him and took a deep breath before announcing, "Perdita Elizabeth Patricia Elaine Reynolds."

Thor looked more than a little taken aback. "How much?"

A giggle escaped her. "There was a squabble over what to name the baby roughly twenty-eight years ago. My mother's sister, Perdita Elizabeth, and my father's sister, Patricia Elaine, both wanted the honor. They were both spinsters, and were mortal enemies from what I've heard; they both died while I was in my teens. The argument became so violent that my parents combined the names, literally flipping a coin to decide what came first. *Then* there was a threatened bloodbath over what to call me. One of my aunts—I don't know which, since both later claimed the inspiration—realized that the first letter of each name, with an extra *P* arbitrarily added, spelled Pepper. I've been called that ever since."

"Perdita," Thor mused. "That's not English."

"No. Latin or Greek. It means 'the lost one.' "

Thor stared laughing. "And you claim to be ordinary! Lord, Pepper, you've been unique from the moment of birth!"

Gazing into his smiling gray eyes, Pepper thought suddenly, *I've come home*. And there it was—the answer to the big question. Why him? Because she'd looked into those eyes, and the gooseflesh and thudding heart had whispered *home*. She had known that she loved him; until then she hadn't known why.

The restlessness that had tormented her for years seeped away in that moment. Before meeting him, she had tentatively planned to visit the Australian Outback during the winter and then see Venice in the spring. There was no hankering in her now to see either place.

Thor, his amusement fading away, saw something different in her violet eyes. A glow that was soft and deep and strangely mysterious. And it wasn't until he heard his own voice speaking that he realized something inside himself recognized that look.

"I can't ask you to break your rules," he said huskily.

"You don't have to." Pepper felt herself smiling, and knew that there was nothing of defeat in it. "I want permanence, Thor. But I know how to live for today. It'll be enough."

"Will it?"

"It'll have to be. Besides, I learned a long time ago that sometimes rules have to be broken. There's just no other way of dealing with them."

"Pepper—"

"Have you ever been seduced?" she asked seriously.

He blinked. "That's . . . that's a loaded question."

"No, I mean, really. Have you ever been seduced?"

"No. No, I haven't."

Slipping her hand from his, she reached out with both to begin slowly and steadily unbuttoning his flannel shirt. "Well . . . there's a first time for everything, or so they say."

Thor was silent and still through three buttons, his eyes locked with hers. "You don't know what you're doing," he breathed finally, his hands catching her wrists in a gentle grip.

Pepper chose deliberately to misunderstand him. "Well, I admit that it's not something I've done before, but I've heard that every woman's a harlot way down deep. I think that's true; I don't feel at all like myself at the moment."

The hands on her wrists didn't attempt to stop her as her fingers continued their task. Instead, they slid up her arms slowly until they came to rest on the delicate bones of her shoulders. His fingers moved slightly, and she could feel the warmth of them through her own flannel shirt.

Pepper's fingers reached the button just above his belt and fumbled suddenly, becoming awkward and uncertain. *If he doesn't help me out,* she thought a little wildly, *I'll never forgive him!*

Whether he sensed her sudden confusion or simply lost patience himself, Thor did help her out. With an odd rough sound that seemed to come from deep inside his chest, he pulled her abruptly against him, his mouth finding hers in a surge of compulsive need.

Her hands slid slowly up his chest, feeling the rough brush of the dark gold mat of hair and the tautening muscles beneath. All her senses came almost painfully alive, sharpened, keen. The tangy scent of his after-shave, the crackle of the fire in the hearth, the hot demand of his lips, the thudding rhythm of his heart, her heart—all filled her being.

She rose up on her knees against him, her fingers tangled in his thick copper-gold hair, her mouth returning fiery demand for fiery demand and adding a helpless plea. She felt her breasts swell and harden against his chest, felt the fierce possession of his hands sliding down her back to her hips. And a reckless, desperate need flooded her veins with molten fury.

Thor's lips finally left hers, and she allowed her eyes to drift open, feeling boneless as he rose and lifted her into his arms in one smooth motion. She kept her arms locked around his neck, gazing into the silvery sheen of his eyes for a long moment. Then her arms tightened and she buried her face briefly in the crook of his neck. She felt his rough breath stirring the hair piled loosely on top of her head.

"Pepper . . ." His voice was hoarse, driven. "If you're not sure . . ."

Her head lifted, violet eyes soft and impossibly deep. "Make love with me, Thor," she whispered. "I need you."

He kissed her briefly, his lips hard and possessive, then turned and carried her toward the stairs. As he started up them Pepper looked back over his shoulder and saw the dogs still in the den. Both pairs of canine eyes were watching their exit, but neither dog attempted to follow them.

How tactful, Pepper thought vaguely, then dismissed the dogs from her mind and concentrated on the feeling of being carried in a man's arms—this man's arms—as though she weighed nothing. Instead of feeling helpless, she felt strangely cared-for and cherished.

Thor carried her down the hall to his bedroom, going through the open door and kicking it shut behind them with one foot. He set her gently on her feet beside the bed and bent to turn on the lamp on the nightstand. As the lamp's soft glow spread over them and the huge four-poster bed, he straightened and looked down at her, his hands lifting to surround her face.

Pepper met his searching gaze with no hesitation, no uncertainty in her own eyes. And when his lips returned to claim hers, her instant and total response laid to rest any question he might have had about whether or not she wanted to make love. The probing of his tongue was answered by her own, her need echoed his, her desire matched his flame for flame.

His hands dropped to the buttons of her shirt,

unsteady, impatient. The shirt was pushed off her shoulders as his mouth left hers to feather a string of kisses down her throat and along her collarbone, and Pepper flung the shirt aside to free her own hands. She tugged his shirt free of the jeans, helping him to shrug it off and let it fall to join hers on the floor. She nudged her loafers off, managing somehow to remove her socks as well, then stepped out of the jeans after he'd unfastened them and pushed them down over her hips.

Immediately her hands found his belt, unfastening it with unconscious familiarity. She slid the zipper down, and was on the point of pushing the jeans down over his hips when he groaned softly and brushed her hands aside. Obviously impatient, he stripped the remainder of his garments off, his eyes never leaving hers.

Absorbed, utterly unselfconscious, Pepper watched him undress. She thought dimly that he did indeed look like a god there in the lamplight; like a proud and pagan figure etched by the golden glow of a long-ago fire. And when he stood before her at last as raw and vital as man was intended to be, she was hardly aware of speaking.

"I knew that towel was a crime."

A curious expression that was half laughter and half passion lit his silvery eyes. "I wondered what you were thinking that night," he murmured huskily, stepping toward her. "You kept looking away from me."

Pepper caught her breath as his big hands began to smooth away her delicate underthings. "It frightened me," she gasped softly. "What I was feeling frightened me. It was too sudden; it happened too fast. . . ."

Thor looked down at her as the last scrap of satin

and lace dropped to the thick pile carpet, his eyes flashing silver fire and then darkening to a stormy slate-gray. "And now?" he breathed, his hands finding her tiny waist and drawing her to him with torturing slowness.

"I'm not frightened now." The words were throaty, filled with longing. Her arms slid around his waist as she closed the distance between them fiercely. "This is right, so right."

He caught his breath sharply, bending his head to find her lips with blind urgency. "God, you're beautiful," he muttered against her mouth. "I'm almost afraid to hold you, almost afraid you'll disappear when I touch you."

"I'm flesh and blood, Thor." Her hands molded the rippling muscles of his back wonderingly. "I'm real . . . a woman. Make me your woman, Thor."

Groaning, Thor reached around her to fling back the covers on the wide bed, then lifted her easily and placed her in its center, following her down immediately. Trapping her restless legs with one of his own, he raked gentle fingers through her silvery hair, sending pins flying, then spread gleaming strands across the pillow. His hands slid down her back as her arms locked around his neck, his lips trailing fire down her throat.

One hand stroked slowly up her rib cage, finding and surrounding her engorged breast. His thumb teased gently, rhythmically, until a hardened bud rose in taut awareness and pleaded for a more intimate caress.

Pepper felt an animal-like whimper rise in her throat as his mouth closed over the aching nipple, then was unaware of the sound when his swirling tongue sent shivers coursing through her body. Her nails dug into the taut muscles of his shoulders. She couldn't be still, couldn't bear to be still; fire was lancing through every cell, every nerve.

Her hands slid up to tangle in his hair, holding him closer as his mouth lavished attention on one breast and then the other. She could hear her own panting, shallow breathing, could feel her heart thundering in runaway need.

"Thor . . ."

"You're beautiful," he rasped against her flesh, teeth nipping gently, then tongue soothing. "God, how I need you!"

His caresses seared the sensitive flesh below her breasts, moved lower, and lower still. Pepper felt his fingers probing erotically, then the hot brush of his lips, and her senses spiraled crazily. Behind her closed eyelids, colors whirled in a kaleidoscope of passion, and a moan ripped its way from the deepest part of her.

Something grew within her, winding tighter and tighter, until she knew that it had to snap. It was hot and cold, sharp and dull, aching with a pain that was a pleasure almost too great to bear. Like a snowball or fireball rolling downhill, it gathered speed and size and filled her with its image, yet left her achingly empty.

"Thor!" Her voice vibrated with a pleading quality. She heard herself as though it were someone else and wondered vaguely at the desperation in that woman's voice. "Please, Thor . . ."

Her lashes, impossibly heavy, lifted as he rose above her, and desire-drugged violet eyes gazed up at him. She saw his lean face taut and masklike in an intolerable need, saw the slate-gray eyes flashing sparks of silver fire. And she saw the hesitation there, the uncertainty, and understood even before he spoke.

"I don't want to hurt you," he whispered raggedly, the words torn from him in his urgency.

Pepper pulled his head down, feeling the tension in him. "You won't," she murmured huskily against his mouth. "You won't hurt me. Love me, Thor—I need you so much!"

With a strange, rough sound from deep in his chest, Thor kissed her hungrily, fiercely. His mouth possessed before his body did, both making her his for all time.

Pepper felt him come to her as though he belonged to her, their bodies fitting as though time itself had decreed it. Her eyes widened, startled at the primitive feeling of being known, totally and completely, for the first time in her life. A little cry of surprise escaped her, surprise and wonderment, and her arms tightened around him in a new and instinctive possessiveness.

As if the act of possession itself were enough, Thor was still for a moment, gazing deeply and searchingly into her eyes. The touch of anxiety in his own eyes faded as she smiled and lifted her head to kiss him, and their lips clung together for a timeless second of eternity.

When Thor began to move, his gentleness and care touched Pepper almost unbearably. Knowledge welled up out of instinct as her body responded to his, matching his rhythm, possessing him as utterly as he possessed her. The hovering tension began to build again, winding itself tighter and tighter, a critical mass that had to find release. It gripped their bodies, driving them relentlessly, compelling them as if they were senseless moths to a fiery death. And the flame was too strong to resist, engulfing them both in an eruption that paralyzed their bodies and cauterized their senses. . . .

"Who," Thor demanded in a voice that sounded a single breath away from exhaustion, "seduced who?"

"Whom," Pepper murmured, snuggling a bit closer to his side and smiling with sleepy contentment.

"The question stands." He reached down to pull the covers up over them both, patting her hip along the way.

Pepper smothered a yawn against the warm flesh of his neck. "Why don't we just call it a joint effort, hmmm?"

"Suits me." He was silent for a long moment, one hand playing almost compulsively with her hair as though he couldn't stop touching her. When he finally spoke again, his voice was very quiet. "Have you caught me, Diana?"

She lifted her head, gazing at him with eyes that were still glowing softly. "You know I haven't."

Thor met her steady gaze for a moment, his own silvery eyes darkening with some kind of conflict. His hand cupped the nape of her neck and drew her forward, and he kissed her forehead softly before pressing her head gently down on his shoulder.

Troubled, Pepper moved even closer, needing to let him know that it was all right, that she understood. "I meant what I said before," she told him softly. "I can live for today, Thor. Don't worry about me."

"I have to." His arm tightened around her almost fiercely. "I have to worry, Pepper. Especially now."

She lifted her head again, holding the hand that had been stroking her hair. "No." A frown flitted across her face and was gone. "Thor, I'm a grown woman, and I've been responsible for my own actions for a long time. So if you're feeling responsible—well, don't."

His eyes were restless on her face. "There could be—"

"Repercussions?" She smiled a little and shook her head. "Not unless I'm one of the few women the Pill likes to trick. The doctor put me on birth control when I was sixteen. You know, my adventurous life-style and all that."

"Oh."

Pepper wondered suddenly why she had the feeling that her remarks had disappointed him. Was he, she wondered dimly, looking for an excuse to prolong their relationship? Did he *want* to be boxed in, with no other alternative? She wondered about his rules and what had written them.

The thought of having to leave him someday—perhaps soon—tortured her, but Pepper was determined that she wouldn't use a single "feminine" weapon to hold him. He'd be hers by *choice* or not at all. That fierce determination helped her to close the door on tomorrow.

"So you don't have to be responsible for me," she told him again quietly.

His restless eyes continued to search her own. "You told me to make you my woman," he said slowly.

Pepper hesitated, then nodded. "I'm your woman as long as you want me," she said with a simple, proud dignity.

Something like awe flickered in Thor's eyes, but

his lips twisted slightly. "But I'm not to feel responsible for you?"

She tried to make him understand. "Thor, I think most women resent that phrase *belong to* because they've never had a chance to belong to themselves. They go from being somebody's daughter to somebody's wife to somebody's mother; they're never just themselves. But I *have* been just me. I've lived alone and taken care of myself. I've belonged to me.

"Don't you see, Thor? I belong to you now, not because you take, but because I give. It was my choice. You're not responsible for that; you're not responsible for me."

He sighed roughly. "So I just accept the . . . the gift and offer nothing in return?"

Pepper pulled herself forward far enough to kiss him. "Thor, stop feeling guilty," she chided gently. "I don't regret a thing; don't make me regret."

Thor hugged her suddenly, a rueful, half painful apology in his eyes. "I'm sorry, be—" He broke off abruptly, then went on so quickly that she wasn't sure he'd started to say something else. "I'm sorry, Pepper. If I had the sense God gave a mushroom, I'd be grateful that you see everything in black and white. If you've no complaints about this relationship, I don't suppose I should question it. And since you're satisfied . . ." He sent her a rather deceptively casual look.

She was smiling faintly. "I'm not going to fall into *that* trap," she told him wryly.

He grinned, honestly amused. "You'd think I'd have learned by now not to fish with you," he remarked in a dry tone.

"You'd think."

Still amused, but with a spark of puzzlement in

his eyes, he studied her. "You're not about to pin me down, are you, Pepper?"

"No."

"Giving me enough rope to hang myself?"

"No."

He lifted an eyebrow at her. "If I told you to leave right now?"

"I'd leave. Right now."

"Without a single recrimination?"

"Not a word."

"Or a tear?"

She was still smiling. "You wouldn't see one."

"You'd just go?"

"I'd pack my things and go." Her eyes were calm and honest.

Thor did an abrupt about-face. "You don't have to sound so damn eager about it," he grumbled morosely.

Pepper started to laugh, wondering if he were half serious and yet realizing that she couldn't probe. The mood between them had lightened, and it had to remain light, she knew, or they'd get bogged down and begin heading toward an ending neither was ready to face yet.

"That wasn't eagerness," she told him solemnly. "That was sweet, womanly compliance with the master's wishes."

He brightened. "Oh, am I the master?"

"Don't let it go to your head."

"Just what kind of authority do I have?"

"Ultimate. Within reason," she responded promptly.

"That's a contradiction in terms."

"Not in my dictionary, it isn't."

"Maybe you'd better explain my authority, then," Thor demanded playfully.

"Don't tell me to shine your shoes."

"I see. Can I tell you to cook for me?"

"Yes. But if you say please, it'll taste better."

"Ah. Would you—uh—dance for me?"

"You have the heart of a Turk."

"I beg your pardon?"

"Harems."

"Uh. The question stands."

"Depends on the dance. And how you 'tell' me to do it."

"I begin to see what you meant by 'within reason.' "

"I thought you'd get it eventually."

"Request rather than command."

"I'm funny that way."

"I should throw away my bullhorn and whip, eh?"

"I would."

"Mmm. Diana?"

"Yes, Thor of the mighty hammer?"

"I have a request."

"Remember to say please."

Thor whispered a few words into her ear, and Pepper's expression was a bit dazed when she lifted her head.

"At least you said please," she mumbled.

It was a long while later when Thor's long arm reached to turn out the lamp on the nightstand. Pepper cuddled closer to him, eyes closed, her smile still a bit dazed. "Vitamin E?" she murmured in sleepy interrogation.

"Wheaties," Thor murmured, and pulled the covers up over them both.

• • •

Pepper dreamed of bees buzzing in her ear and automatically lifted a hand to shoo the pesky insects away. But her hand encountered a powerful masculine arm just as the buzzing stopped, and she decided muzzily to let Thor deal with intruding bugs. Drifting deeper into sleep, she thought she heard his deep voice talking to the bugs in low tones, but that was ridiculous because, Pepper told herself, people didn't talk to bugs.

Time passed, but Pepper didn't know how much. She just knew that something was wrong, something was missing, and the coldness and loneliness of its absence woke her up. She opened her eyes suddenly, wide-awake and disturbed. The room was dark, the luminous face of the clock on the nightstand proclaiming it to be just after four in the morning.

And except for her the huge four-poster bed was empty.

Pepper sat up and looked around. The door to the bathroom was open, and no light was coming from within; the door to the hallway was barely open, and only the dim hallway light was visible. She slid her hand across the bed beneath the covers, feeling the lingering warmth of his presence. He couldn't have been gone long then.

Where had he gone?

Not one to sit and wonder, Pepper slipped from the bed, not bothering with the lamp to find her flannel shirt still lying on the floor. She pulled it on and began to button it, opening the door to the hall and pausing for a moment to listen intently. Dimly she could make out a low voice coming from the den.

She went down the hall to the stairs, walking

lightly on bare feet, then down the stairs and to the doorway of the den. Thor was sitting half turned away from her, talking on the phone. He was completely dressed, and a jacket lay on the couch beside him. His face, revealed to her in profile, was expressionless except for a certain remoteness, and his voice was calm and level.

"Venezuela. Yes. No, they didn't know. Get the jet ready. I'll be there within an hour. Right." He hung up the receiver.

Staring across at him, Pepper's thoughts screamed inside her head. *Not tonight! Oh, please, not tonight! Not when it's so new and we're afraid to touch it.* . . .

Nine

Thor looked up and toward the doorway, and saw her standing there. She was wearing only a flannel shirt that barely covered the tops of her thighs, looking more sexy, he thought, than nine out of ten women could look in sequins and feathers. Her hair was a little mussed from sleep, but the wide, curiously bottomless violet eyes held no drowsiness; they looked at him with a gentle inquiry that held only as much curiosity as he would be willing to satisfy.

He wanted to move, wanted desperately to cross the room to her and hold her. Wanted to explain what he didn't have words for. Wanted to find words for the feelings tormenting him. Wanted to smile at her and tell her that everything would be all right.

He looked away.

"I have to leave." *Beloved*.

She came slowly into the room, halting at the end of the couch and continuing to watch him steadily. "Do you know when you'll be back?" she asked softly.

"No. Not really." *Beloved.*

Still steady, she asked, "Do you want me to be here when you get back?"

His gaze moved swiftly back to hers. "Yes." *Beloved!*

An odd little sigh, almost soundless, came from her lips. "I'll feed Lucifer for you while you're gone."

"Thank you." So stiff, so brusque. *Oh, beloved. . . .*

He got to his feet and shrugged into the jacket as though the task demanded his utmost attention. He didn't look at her.

"Anything else you'd like for me to do?"

Tell me you'll miss me! "No."

She nodded slightly, and only the sudden clenching of one small fist at her side showed him that she wasn't as calm as she looked. He stared at the fist for a moment, then his gaze moved upward to her grave face. For an eternal second there was utter silence in the room. Even the two dogs, lying side by side in front of the cold hearth, neither moved, nor made a sound.

Thor started to step past her and head for the front door, but then something snapped inside of him. He turned suddenly and caught her in his arms, holding her with all the desperation he felt inside.

The releif of his sudden embrace was staggering to Pepper, and her arms slid beneath his jacket and around his waist eagerly. She could sense the emotions tearing at him, feel them in the tautness of his body and the strength of his arms, but understanding eluded her. She knew only that he was leaving her, and the fear that he would go without even touching her had brought agony.

He turned her face up with hands that weren't quite steady, his lips claiming hers with a ferocity that branded her as his—a strange, despairing possessiveness that seemed to deny its own existence.

And then he was gone.

Her lips throbbing, senses and thoughts in a whirl, she listened to the roar of the Corvette die away in the distance. Then a light—a candle—flickered to life somewhere in the back of her mind. It lit the area of darkness she had yet to find her way through, showing her a possible answer to the riddle of Thor's rules.

Pepper stood there for a long moment, and gradually everything began to make sense. Thor's reluctance to make a commitment, his constraint in the matter of his job, the impersonal house.

The house. She turned and left the den, spending the next half hour going through the house, room by room. She looked this time with eyes not searching for clues, but for confirmation. And she found it. Returning to the den, she sank down in a chair and stared into the cold, blackened remains of last night's fire in the hearth.

Granted, it was a guess. She could very well be wrong. But Pepper didn't think so. It explained the dichotomy. The man possessing the innate ability to care and to care deeply, to be sensitive. The man who avoided commitments, refused ties, and hated good-byes. It explained him.

Her puzzle was assembling itself with dizzying haste, the pieces falling neatly into place, and she was almost certain that the emerging picture was the right one.

What was his job? It occasionally took him out of the country—he'd mentioned Venezuela on the telephone. He'd told the person on the other end of the line to "get the jet ready." To Pepper's sharp mind that didn't necessarily mean what it would have meant to eight out of ten women—wealth; to her it meant haste, speed. Thor had been called to Venezuela, and he'd had to get there fast.

The job was dangerous. That much she was intuitively and instinctively certain of. And specialized. A man wouldn't be asked to leave his own country with all speed in order to handle a run-of-the-mill problem. Jean had offhandedly mentioned that Thor had been in Mexico at the same time she herself had been last year. Mexico? She'd read the papers; what had been happening in Mexico during that time? And then she remembered.

An oil well fire.

It had been a big one, she remembered. Three wells within spitting distance of one another, and all burning. And the situation had been complicated by the presence of terrorists who'd been determined to let the wells burn. The military called in . . . The terrorists fading into the hills and taking potshots at anything that moved . . . Valuable crude oil burning away . . . And they'd called in—

A highly specialized team of firefighters! An American team! Men—she couldn't recall mention of women—trained to extinguish oil fires, chemical fires, any kind of more than usually dangerous fire where specialized knowledge was called for, technical skill demanded, and sheer raw courage—or stupidity—was required.

There was only a handful of such teams, Pepper was sure. A high-risk profession, often taking its members into remote areas and demanding of them the limit of endurance. And with present-day fears of terrorist takeovers, revolutionary coups, and "small" wars, any one of which could easily involve a very valuable oil field, it was a very dangerous profession.

She could be wrong about it, of course. But it seemed right.

And there was more to it all—she *felt* it! More to Thor, more behind his avoidance of commitment than dangerous work. She fiercely put from her mind the knowledge that he was, even now, on his way to carry on that dangerous work. Could it be . . . ? No. No, just because she was sensitive to that, just because *she'd* been . . .

But it fell into place so neatly, so logically. His father had . . . and his mother? And perhaps because of that, he'd . . .

It angered her. In fact, it made her damn furious! Because she could have been fighting it all this time instead of shadowboxing in the dark. And the worst part was that she *understood*.

If she was right about it all, it was uncanny, really, her upbringing and his so similar at the roots: Both had watched a father going into danger and a mother's terror. And from that common experience, each had evolved their separate and curiously dissimilar rules.

She was a gambler who knew better than to believe in certainty but wanted permanence. Brave, with an intelligent courage that saw the risk before taking the chance, Pepper had seen life in all its realities, all its painful, tawdry, reckless uncertainty. And she had felt the curious lure of danger, the excitement of challenge. She understood it because she'd inherited her father's courageous spirit, had absorbed the tragic regrets of the mother who had learned too late of years shadowed by crippling fear.

And so Pepper had promised herself never to look back with regret. She didn't shrink from danger or avoid risk. She reached out to people, gathering them around her happily and naming them friends. She satisfied her nearly insatiable curiosity, whether the result was a visit to an X-rated night spot in Europe or a period of study under the amused eye of a disreputable cardsharp.

She put down roots, however temporarily, wherever she went. She forged ties to people and places and things. Her friends were her friends, hostages to fortune with her knowledge and acceptance. And if fortune demanded a price to be paid, she would pay it then. She would not—*would not*—love one whit less just because that love could well be held, like the sword of Damocles, over her head one day.

And Thor? The root they had in common, she thought, had branched off in a different direction for him. He'd probably inherited a love of danger, of risk, from his father, and that recklessness was at odds with the sensitive man who'd watched his mother's fear. And being the man he was, Thor had chosen not to inflict that fear on another. He'd decided to go his own way alone.

It explained the house. Beautiful, a comfortable place to return to, but containing no memories. If he were to be suddenly wiped out of existence, there would be nothing in this house to cause anyone pain. It was impersonal with studied, deliberate care.

It explained Cody, the friend who was closer than Thor realized. Cody, who saw and respected the shield Thor carried to protect others from caring about him, and who came around anyway. The man who understood Thor and took care never to let him see that he *was* a hostage to fortune, took care never to let him know that a friend worried over him.

Because he'd have no hostages to fortune, and be no hostage himself—not Thor, the god of thunder—the reckless man could not be less than he was. And the sensitive man, held captive by his own choice, wouldn't let himself care.

Pepper wondered painfully what it had cost him. He was, she thought, a remarkable man not to have become embittered, not to have fallen back on sarcasm and coldness to shore up his shield. But he hadn't. He was quick and witty and humorous—at least with her.

And that, she realized, was the final piece of the puzzle falling neatly into place.

With her . . .

If she and Thor had met in some more conventional way, she would have seen him that first time with his shield up, his defenses strong. Instead, she had caught him off guard. The newspaper ad and then the story behind it had intrigued him, and he had gone to meet her against his better judgment. Their meeting . . . Brutus's attack . . . Impossible to be on guard with absurdity erupting all around you! And, the shield having dropped in surprise, it could never be raised quite so high again. Not with her.

And Pepper—blindly feeling her way—out of instinct or intuition or sheer damn dumb luck had stumbled on exactly the right methods to keep that shield partly lowered. She had challenged him, and with a streak of recklessness as wide as her own, he had accepted the challenge. It had amused him at first, she thought, intrigued him. The chase. But the chase had rapidly grown larger than both of them, and they had become caught up in it.

He had been a man alone. His housekeeper of five years had been a relative stranger to him, his home impersonal, his life ordered and limited. His only tie had been to a stallion named Lucifer who'd loved him and only him, and in spite of himself Thor had let himself care.

Lucifer was, perhaps, a beginning. A chink in the shield. And then she had barged into his life, bringing with her a neurotic Doberman, an attack-trained Chihuahua with inquisitive habits . . . and a puzzle. She had chipped away at his shield cheerfully, never realizing that he wasn't running from her at all, but from images burned in his mind.

Brutally abrupt good-byes. Fear-tainted absences. Desperate worry. And finally, the image that would haunt the kind of man he was: a woman in widow's black weeping in a darkened room.

Hostages to fortune. Himself a hostage to someone else's fortune, and he wouldn't be that, never be that, never that.

"Dammit," Pepper said, startling herself. She looked around, blinking, and realized that day had arrived while she'd been lost in thought. The dogs were quiet, heads lifted and eyes fixed expectantly on her. They're hungry, she thought vaguely. Breakfast time.

Then she heard the sound of Jean's VW, and the dogs raced to the front door to greet her. Pepper sat where she was, saying a quiet string of swear words she'd learned in various languages. Damn the man, anyway. How to convince him that he was already her hostage to fortune and always would be? And judging by that embrace just before he'd gone, that she was his hostage to fortune whether he knew it . . . or wanted it?

"He's gone?"

Pepper looked across to the doorway, meeting Jean's eyes. "He's gone. Venezuela, I think."

Jean nodded slightly, watching the younger woman with sympathy. "It's usually only a few days," she volunteered quietly.

"Yes." Pepper asked no questions, knowing that the housekeeper would understand. She'd hear the story from Thor or from no one. Period.

"I'll fix breakfast," Jean murmured. "And feed the dogs."

Pepper shook her head slightly. "I'm not hungry."

"You have to eat."

Looking across the room to meet concerned, motherly eyes, Pepper couldn't help but smile. "Okay. I'll . . . I'll go upstairs and get dressed."

That day passed, then a second and a third. Pepper groomed her clients during the day, helped Jean experiment with "foreign" culinary fare, and took care of Thor's horse and her own pets.

It was the nights that were bad. Jean had offered that first night to stay later than usual, but Pepper knew that she had a husband waiting for her at home, and refused to allow it. Any one—or two—of her friends would have been delighted to come and stay, but Pepper didn't even consider that.

She waited alone.

Watching television, knitting, reading, all were means to fill the time. A third night of automatically knitting while staring at the television produced a colorful afghan, which she defiantly tossed over the back of the couch.

It wasn't fear that tortured her during those endless nights. It was uncertainty. She couldn't know, after all, that Thor was even then in danger. She couldn't know. Except that she did. Her uncertainty, though, was all wrapped up in his work and his rules.

What right did she have to tell Thor that he was wrong about avoiding commitments? She had seen how fear could batter the mind and twist the spirit; she understood his reasoning. But she still thought he was wrong. And no special wisdom told her that.

It was just that she loved him.

His absence gave Pepper the time she needed to gather her thoughts and emotions and examine them as objectively as she could. And as the days passed she realized it wasn't only because she loved him and wanted to share his life that she believed his rules wrong. He was cheating himself, she knew, and cheating others as well. And no matter what happened between them, she meant to make him see that.

Pepper was curled up on the couch in the den watching a movie on television when she heard the Corvette. It would have been her fifth night alone.

As the dogs rushed to the front door she sat up slowly and used the remote control to turn off the television. Nervously smoothing the fine silk of her blue gown and negligee, Pepper steeled herself to stay put and not rush to greet him. She wanted to, God knew, but she was afraid. Because, while she'd had time to think during these last days, he probably had too. And she didn't know what conclusions he'd reached.

So she stayed put and listened to her heart thundering in her ears and the sound of his voice as he greeted the eagerly welcoming dogs. It wasn't until he spoke directly to her from the doorway that Pepper rose slowly to her feet.

"Well, two out of three's not bad, I guess."

She stared across the room at him, feeding the hunger inside of her with the sight of him. Dressed almost exactly the same as when he'd left, he shrugged his jacket off and tossed it on a chair, revealing a casual flannel shirt and jeans. He looked tired, she thought, but was blessedly whole and unhurt, and she took an instinctive step toward him.

But as he stepped into the room and into the light, she saw the look in his eyes and halted. She swallowed hard and forced herself to respond easily to his comment and not to the look that told her the ending was, perhaps, in sight.

"I didn't think you'd want a clinging sort of woman."

"What sort of woman are you, Pepper? No curiosity? No questions?"

"Both," she responded quietly. "I'll ask the questions if you're ready to answer. Are you, Thor?"

"Yes." He walked abruptly over to the window, showing her only a sharply etched profile against the blackened glass.

Pepper sat down on the edge of the couch, watching him. She took a deep breath, wondering if she hoped or dreaded her guesses to be confirmed. "Then tell me about your job."

He smiled a little, wryly. "Right to the heart of the matter. That's my Pepper."

"Tell me, Thor."

"I'm a partner in a small company," he told her quietly. "We specialize in dealing with fires. Oil and chemical fires; the kind that ordinary firemen just aren't trained or equipped to deal with. We fly all over the world, to remote areas and into cities and put out the fires. Sometimes we deal with deliberate sabotage, or duck bullets in some idiotic brush war, or fight diplomatic or bureaucratic red tape."

"And that's why you . . . you wrote your rules?" she questioned, sure now of the answer.

"My father and his partner started the company." Thor's voice was flat, tight. "My mother loved my father very much. When I got old enough to understand that—really understand it—I saw what it did to her. Having to say good-bye to him, time after time, knowing that each time could be for good. It made her old before the years caught up with her."

"And your father?" Pepper asked quietly.

"Dad." Thor smiled faintly. "He loved her. But this business . . . well, it gets into the blood. The challenge, I guess. The danger. He tried to spend time behind a desk—for her. But it didn't work for him."

Pepper waited silently.

"He was killed," Thor said abruptly. "An accident; they're common in this business. The explosives were unstable, more so than normal. He was too near the blast."

"I'm sorry."

Thor nodded slightly, then went on in the same flat tone. "Mom died a year later. Her heart, the doctors said. I think they were more right than they knew."

"And you went on with the business."

"I went on." He shrugged slightly, the movement rough. "Like I said—it gets into the blood. My father couldn't sit behind a desk. I can't either."

"No commitments," Pepper said softly.

Thor looked at her steadily. "After watching my mother die for twenty-five years, fear eating at her like a cancer? No. I can take the risk; I'll be responsible for me. But I won't torture another human being."

"Do you think you can make that choice?" she asked flatly.

Thor was silent, staring out the window again. The back turned to her was stiffly held, tension evident.

"Do you?" she repeated fiercely.

"It's my choice to make," he said almost inaudibly. "God knows, there are enough victims in the world; I won't help add to the list."

"You're suffering under an excess of nobility, Thor," she told him, letting scorn color her voice. He turned suddenly to face her—which was what she had wanted—and she went on quickly.

"It was never your choice, Thor! And, however this little game of ours ends, win, lose, or draw, I'll make you understand that!"

"Pepper—"

"All right, your mother couldn't take worrying about her husband; *my* mother couldn't take it either. Their men went into danger and it nearly destroyed them—did destroy your mother in the end. Well, it wouldn't destroy *me*! Not because danger frightens me any less, or because I'd care any less, but because I can handle it."

He looked puzzled. "Your mother . . . ?"

"My father was a cop." Pepper looked at Thor steadily. "He didn't have to be; his family was wealthy. But Dad was a cop down to his socks and through to his soul; it was in him to care about people, and he hated injustice. He loved his work. He also loved my mother. It took him two years to talk her into marrying him; she was terrified of being a cop's wife.

"Like your father, mine offered to try sitting behind a desk. But Mom . . . was strong in some ways. She knew that she had no real right to use the emotional power she had over him. He would have quit if she'd asked; she never did. And she loved him too much to walk away from him.

"So I went through the same thing as you, Thor. Whenever he was on duty, I watched her jump when the phone rang, watched her pale when someone knocked on the door. I saw her cling to him that extra second before he left in the morning, and that extra second when he came home— safe. At first I was too young to understand or see anything out of the ordinary; I thought every kid's mother was nervous whenever Dad worked.

"Then I got older. And I saw then. I saw her bite her nails to the quick and pace the floor. I saw her watch television or listen to the radio with this terrible dread hanging over her if there was a report of police in a dangerous situation. And I got used to Dad calling her immediately because he'd known how it tortured her."

Thor had come forward, his strong hands resting on the back of a chair, almost gripping it, as he listened. "What happened?"

"He was killed." Pepper smiled a twisted smile. "But there was an irony about it. You see, Dad didn't die in the line of duty. His death was due to one of those senseless 'accidents' that fill up statistical sheets. He'd driven down to the local market for something—I forget what. A drunken driver swung wide on a turn and plowed into Dad's car head-on. He was killed instantly. The other man walked away."

She shook her head slightly. "We were at home waiting dinner for him when someone knocked on the door. It was funny; when Mom went to answer and saw Dad's partner standing there, she didn't suspect a thing. Dad wasn't on duty, you see. He hadn't even taken his gun with him."

"It must have been rough on both of you," Thor murmured, wondering at the uncanny similarity of their pasts.

"It was." Pepper lifted her chin and met his eyes levelly. "But both of us learned something very important. My first reaction was about what yours had been, that I'd never go through what Mom had, or allow anyone else to suffer because of me. Mom grew stronger. Not because the worst had happened and she didn't have to be afraid anymore, but because she realized how fear had cheated her all those years. She saw that their life together could have been so much fuller and happier if she'd only lived each day as it came instead of constantly dreading something she had no control over.

"And she made me understand that. She taught me that the worst thing anyone can do in this life is to regret—anything. Life's too short for that. Mom found out too late, but I didn't. I've been reckless more than once, and I've taken chances, but

I've never regretted, Thor. And I don't ever intend to."

His hands tightened on the back of the chair. "And I don't intend to watch anyone suffer because of me."

Pepper laughed suddenly, a wry sound. "You believe that you can prevent others from caring about you? What about Jean? After five years d'you believe she thinks of you only as an employer, that she doesn't know you inside out? That she wouldn't feel grief if something happened to you? And what about Cody? He was your best friend until your father was killed, and then you shut him out. But he keeps coming around, doesn't he? He keeps coming around because you're his friend and he cares about you.

"And Lucifer? Oh, he's just a horse . . . but we both know animals feel. He loved you in spite of yourself, and you couldn't just walk away from that. And the dogs. Thor, both of them looked everywhere for you while you were gone, did you know that? They missed you."

She rose and went over to stand by the chair, staring up at him. "Thor, all of us give hostages to fortune, whether we will it or not. It isn't our choice to make. And we're all hostages to someone else's fortune. We can't protect those we care about from things we have no control over. We can't insulate ourselves or them."

"Pepper—"

Reaching up, she placed two fingers lightly across his lips to halt whatever he'd been about to say. "Think about it," she urged quietly. "That's all I'm asking, Thor. If you decide in the end that you'd rather not litter your life with . . . with hostages to fortune, then that's that. I told you I'd know if you took to your heels in earnest."

Her smile was a little twisted. "But you asked me for honesty, so there's something you have to know. If I walked out that door tonight, nothing would change. Like it or not, you're a hostage to someone else's fortune."

He reached out suddenly to pull her against him, his arms wrapping her in a tight bear hug. "When are you going to stop surprising me?" he asked huskily, his chin rubbing slowly in her hair.

Pepper slid her arms around his waist, the feeling of his hard body pressed against hers only beginning to feed her hunger. Instead of answering his murmured question, she asked one of her own. "Do you mind if I cling . . . just a little?"

"I'd need to have my head examined if I did," he whispered, almost to himself.

"Thor?"

"Hmm?"

"Welcome home. I missed you."

He went very still for a moment, then swung her up into his arms and started for the stairs. "I missed you too," he said gruffly.

"Pepper?"

"Hmmm?"

"Will you show me your home-on-wheels tomorrow?"

"If you like."

"I think it's time, don't you?"

"I've just been waiting for you to ask."

"Diana, matchmaker, mender of lonely hearts, goddess of the hunt, how did I manage to stumble across you?"

"You answered an ad in the paper."

He saw Pepper's home the next morning, saw the pieces of the puzzle beginning to fit neatly together. It was all there, as she'd said, but only to those who cared to look and knew what to look for. It was bright and cheerful and cluttered with memories. There were snapshots tacked up everywhere of the friends she'd made all over the world, mementos of the places she'd been.

Ties. Bonds.

Exploring like a cat with Pepper's smiling permission, Thor looked into closets and corners. He found evidence of her competitive spirit in trophies and awards. And he saw that the awards themselves meant little to her, since they were used merely to prop open doors or hold down papers, or were left to gather dust on the top shelf of a closet.

Small, custom-designed, and built-in cases held collections of jade and ivory, cheek-by-jowl with the crayoned drawings of children befriended along the way. Books on every conceivable subject were jammed into bookshelves and piled in corners, topped here and there by battered stuffed animals. A compact stereo system was surrounded by tapes and albums.

From the cheerful clutter emerged a portrait of a woman who made friends and kept them, was intensely curious, competitive out of a love of challenge, had been everywhere—and probably seen everything—and had somehow managed to retain her enthusiasm for everything.

Everything, Thor mused silently, staring around him at her home. That was Perdita

Elizabeth Patricia Elaine Reynolds. Honest, reckless, impulsive, humorous, wise, caring, lively one moment and reflective the next. How many women was she?

As many as I have to be, she'd said.

He looked now at her smiling face, the softly glowing eyes, remembered the night before and a passion matching his own. Like a thorn, she'd worked her way beneath his skin, but, oddly enough, there was no pain. And he wondered if it was too late for her to teach him what he wanted to learn.

He'd shut so much of himself away that he wasn't sure he could ever reach for those feelings again, sort through them, make sense of them. He wanted to reach out to her, but he wasn't sure how. And because she'd never told him what he needed to hear in simple words, he was afraid to try.

"Pepper?"

"Hmm?"

"Your home is . . . beautiful."

"Thank you. I hoped you'd like it."

The days passed, days filled with laughter and companionship. And nights filled with magic. Pepper taught Thor how to groom a hostile poodle, and worked determinedly at making his job a casual topic for conversation. She told him about some of her more absurd experiences and encouraged him to talk about his life before she'd landed in the middle of it. She played the piano for him, discovering that the instrument had been his mother's and that he couldn't play a note.

She cooked for him. She even danced for him.

The dance was one she'd picked up on her travels, and was immediately dubbed the Dance of a Veil-and-a-half by a bemused Thor. It also led to a rather interesting evening.

A week. Two.

Pepper had her own reasons for not telling Thor that she loved him—although she thought that if the man didn't know by now, he was as blind as a bat!—but his continued silence on that subject, and the subject of whether or not they had a future together, unnerved her badly. Both her instincts and intuition failing her, she didn't stop to think that Thor had closed down that part of himself too thoroughly to be easily opened again.

Her only thought was that perhaps he was content with the undefined limits of their relationship.

But Pepper wasn't. True, she'd told Thor in all honesty that she could live for today. But she knew that every day she remained with him would make it that much harder to leave when she had to. And she still felt hope that he wouldn't want her to leave.

Wouldn't *let* her leave. . . .

So, closing her eyes and whispering a devout prayer to the patron saint of lovers, Pepper took the biggest gamble of her life.

Ten

Thor stepped into the living room and halted, a sudden wave of coldness sweeping him from head to toe as he listened to Pepper talking on the phone. He found himself straining to pick up some nuance of hesitation in her tone, some regret . . . something. But her voice was even and unemotional. He could see her profile clearly; it seemed set and determined, and her eyes gazed across the room with a fixed intensity.

"Yes, Mr. Morris, I've talked with Miss James. Yes, I've thought about it, and—I've decided not to take over the business permanently. Yes, I'm . . . sorry too. No, I enjoyed it tremendously. I love animals. Well, I think it's time for me to move on."

For the first time Thor noted a hesitation, a wavering in her voice. But then it was even again.

"Miss James told you about me, eh? Yes, I'm something of a traveler. I'll probably be leaving the country after we get this business taken care of. No, it's just the equipment; I operated out of my . . . my home. If you could arrange to store the equipment somewhere until it's sold . . . ? Yes. No, Monday will be soon enough. I'll bring the books by, and you can make sure that everything is in order. Two o'clock? That's fine. Yes. Yes, I'll be there. Thank you, Mr. Morris. Good-bye."

Pepper cradled the receiver slowly, her gaze still fixed on something that seemed far away and none too happy. Thor saw the worry-stone that had been absent these last weeks in her hand, her thumb moving with a methodical rhythm. Only that movement and the faraway eyes betrayed her.

"You're leaving me," he said suddenly, hoarsely. He slid his hands into the pockets of his jeans as she got up and turned to face him. His hands were shaking, and he didn't want her to see.

Pepper looked across at him for a moment, almost as though he were slowly coming into focus. Then she smiled easily, and he instantly recognized the curtain falling between them.

"I talked to Kristen this afternoon. I charged the call to a credit card, so you won't be billed for it."

"Dammit, Pepper," he muttered, swearing at her trivial aside. But she was going on cheerfully.

"It seems that the English breeder did have something permanent in mind when he swept her off to England; they're getting married in three weeks. And since he has all the grooming equipment he needs, she decided to sell hers. She offered me the business, but I decided to pass. I was just talking to her lawyer to arrange the transfer."

"Why won't you tell me that you love me?" he murmured, hearing the puzzled, raw sound of his own voice.

Pepper turned away suddenly and walked over to the window, staring out as though the distant pastures held a driving interest for her. "I thought I'd go to Australia next," she said lightly, tossing the words over her shoulder. "I've only been there briefly before—flyovers and one-night layovers. I'd like to see the Outback. And kangaroos and koalas in the wild. And then maybe a cruise. I've always loved the sea. I could—"

"Why won't you tell me that you love me?" he repeated fiercely, nothing uncertain about his voice now. He saw the worry-stone still in her hand, still being worried methodically, unconsciously.

"Fifi will be happy with you here. I'll leave Brutus and the van with Mom; I always do when I'm traveling." She went on as though he hadn't spoken, but her voice was strained now, uneven. "Next week probably. My passport's up-to-date, and all my shots."

"*Dammit*, Pepper! Why won't you tell me that you love me?"

She whirled abruptly, showing him a face that was no longer calm. "Because you're not a man to cut notches on your belt!" she told him almost violently. Then she looked down and saw the worry-stone in her hand, flinging it toward the couch with a muttered curse.

Thor shook his head. "What the hell's that supposed to mean?" he asked roughly.

Pepper crossed her arms across her breasts and met his gaze, in control once more. "If you were that sort of man," she said in a calm voice, "and I told you . . . it would be a sort of trophy for you. You'd look back on it with enjoyment, and a kind of pride. You know"—she smiled crookedly—

"another one bit the dust. Another scalp. Another notch."

"Pepper—"

"But you're not that sort of man," she cut him off flatly. "Don't you see, Thor? It'll be the past. And I'd rather nothing was said that you couldn't forget if you wanted to. Nothing to regret."

Thor moved toward her slowly, taking his hands from his pockets. When he stood before her, he held her eyes steadily with his own. "And what about you?" he asked huskily. "Will you have regrets?"

She shook her head immediately. "No. These past weeks . . . no, I won't have any regrets."

His hands lifted to her shoulders, the thumbs moving over her collarbone with a restless impatience. "Tell me that you love me," he said, his voice dropping to a dark and compelling rumble.

"Thor, don't make this any harder please. I told you that I wouldn't complicate your life. I told you that you wouldn't have to ask me to leave. But I didn't say I'd be happy about it. Don't make me regret."

"Tell me that you love me."

Pepper looked up into his taut face, the determined gray eyes. "Why?" she asked shakily. "You're *not* a man to cut notches in your belt. So why?"

"I have to hear you say it," he told her fiercely.

"You know how I feel." She felt the hands on her shoulders tighten almost convulsively, and saw a muscle leap in his rigidly held jaw. And the nearly drowned hope inside of her surfaced with a breath of new life.

"I have to hear you say it." His voice was ragged,

shaken with a depth of feeling she hadn't dared to hope for.

He watched her face intensely, seeing her steel herself like someone fearing a slap. But when she finally spoke, her voice was quiet and sure, with a certainty that needed no intensity, no emphasis, to prove itself.

"I love you, Thor." She lifted her hands to touch his face, lightly, as if needing a tentative reassurance of reality. "I love you."

Thor saw the glow in her lovely eyes, the expression he'd seen before and never dared put a name to. And the coldness that had held him in its grip from the moment he'd entered the room finally released him. He caught her fiercely in his arms, holding her with a strength just this side of savagery. "God, Pepper! I was so afraid!"

His hands found her face, tilting it up urgently. He kissed her with a curious mixture of passion and tenderness, a delicate high-wire balance she gloried in because it meant that depth of feeling she hadn't dared to hope for. It meant—

"I love you, Pepper," he breathed unsteadily when his lips finally left hers. "I love you with everything inside of me."

She caught her breath, staring up at him, a sense of wonder filling her. The same wonder she saw in his eyes. Wonder and a giddy happiness, and a sense of wholeness she'd never felt before. Her arms slipped around his waist, and she felt the certainty of touching the other half of herself.

"Thor . . ."

His hands still framed her face, warm and strong. "Don't leave," he said huskily. "Stay with me."

She nodded, almost without being aware of

doing so. "Who needs Australia?" she murmured. "Let the Aussies have it."

Thor gazed into the loving depths of her violet eyes, and a quiet laugh escaped him. "You and your chasing! You won after all; I'm trapped."

Pepper carefully stepped back until they were no longer touching. "There's no trap, Thor." She shook her head, smiling. "You're free. Tell me to leave; I'll go. I'm not asking for a ring and a promise."

He reached out to pull her abruptly to him once again. "But I am." His grin was crooked. "A ring and a whole basketful of promises. And I don't give a damn whose idea it was in the beginning."

She smiled up at him, more than content. But his next sober question surprised her; she honestly hadn't expected him to feel the need for a real commitment.

"Marry me?"

Pepper swallowed hard. "Thor, you don't have to marry me. It's enough that you love me." She laughed shakily. "You're *really* breaking your rules!"

"A very wise lady told me once," he said deeply, "that sometimes rules have to be broken. There's just no other way of dealing with them."

"Thor—"

"Marry me, sweetheart. I need you beside me for the rest of our lives. I need your humor and your strength and your intelligence. And most of all I need your love. I need to bind us together with every promise, every thread I can find. And—dammit!—I want it in writing! The kind of writing that you and I understand and believe in, the kind that means forever."

Pepper was vaguely aware that she wasn't

breathing, but it didn't seem to matter very much. She could only gaze up at the man she loved more than life, and feel a deeply grateful awe that somehow—overcoming the stumbling blocks their separate lives had placed between them—they had found one another.

He held her even more firmly, looking down at her with the eyes of a man who'd doubted heaven . . . and found it against all odds. "I'm yours more than my own," he said quietly, roughly. "And I always will be. If you'd walked out that door, part of me would have gone with you. A large part. And I wouldn't have been able to forget even if I'd wanted to. You would have haunted me all the days of my life. Awake and asleep.

"Marry me, beloved. Stay with me . . . forever."

She swallowed again. "You're not worried about—about hostages anymore?"

Thor bent his head to kiss her very gently. "I'll always worry," he murmured. "But the difference is that now I know how empty my life was without them."

"I love you," she whispered, "and I want to be your wife more than anything in the world!"

He held her fiercely. "I hope that means yes," he said unsteadily.

Pepper slid her arms up around his neck, pulling his head down and telling him in the best way she knew that it did indeed mean yes. . . .

It was some hours later and they were lying close together in the big four-poster bed when the conversation became rational again.

"Beloved?"

"Mmm, I just love that," she murmured, moved oddly by his rough-edged endearment; neither of them tossed around endearments lightly. "What is it, darling?"

He drew her a bit nearer. "Would you have left me?"

"I'm glad we didn't have to find out," she said softly.

He chuckled suddenly. "You were gambling, weren't you?"

"Well . . ."

"Oh, Lord. What have I let myself in for?"

Pepper snuggled closer, smiling contentedly. "The biggest poker game of them all, darling."

"With a cardsharp yet!"

"But aren't you glad I've got the winning hand?"

"In this game, beloved, I think we've both won."

"I know we have."

"And all the cards are wild."

"Only one-eyed jacks and deuces, darling."

"And the queen of hearts."

"True. She cheats, you know—the queen of hearts."

"Not a lady at all."

"S'terrible. Just terrible."

"Aces up her sleeves . . ."

"And love in her heart. . . ."

Pepper gave the concoction in the pan a last stir and tasted it critically. "There's *still* something missing," she said to her canine audience, then made a hasty lunge at the large Siamese tom who'd leaped onto the counter. "Not while I'm cooking, Tut!" she said, putting him firmly back onto the floor. "Blasted cat—why'd you have to eat the recipe card, for Pete's sake? Now I'll never know what's missing!"

King Tut cuffed an inquisitive Brutus without malice and then calmly sat down to wash a seal-brown paw.

"Some wedding present you turned out to be," Pepper told him darkly. "Cody and his bright ideas! Fifi, stop trying to wash his ears; you know he doesn't like it." The Doberman retired to a corner with an injured expression after being soundly cuffed by the disdainful cat, and Pepper sighed.

"I live in a nuthouse."

She glanced up at the kitchen clock and felt the warmth of Thor's imminent arrival filling her. Just another few minutes now; he'd called as soon as the jet touched down. One more dangerous assignment completed successfully, she thought, and let her mind wander back over the past year.

Once having taken the plunge, Thor had opened up wonderfully. He'd been concerned at first, she knew, watching her for any signs of the worry and dread both remembered from their respective mothers. But Pepper had been determined not to live in fear, and she hadn't.

And they had discovered that although the leave-takings were never fun, the homecomings had been wonderful. Pepper had worked to turn the house into a home, filling time while Thor's work claimed him and never letting herself brood. There was nothing impersonal about their home now, nothing detached. Houseplants, knitted afghans, photos taken during the last year, and the items collected over Pepper's years of travel now filled the house. The home.

Leaning back against the counter, Pepper absently watched Tut playfully attack Brutus's tail. Thor had been immediately adopted by her friends during the past months, and Pepper had had the pleasure of watching him and Cody become closer.

Cody. Pepper giggled suddenly. She'd have to do something about Cody soon; he'd been footloose and fancy-free too long. He needed a wife to curb his mischievous ways. She thought of the peculiar sculpture that had been his gift on his last visit; he always brought something. The sculpture was a marvelous conversation-starter at parties, since no one seemed to be able to figure out what it was. It now graced the coffee table in their den, and Tut seemed strangely fascinated by it.

Still, Cody needed a home of his own. Pepper thought for a moment of the few unattached friends she had. Then she began to smile. Brooke, of course, and why hadn't she thought of her sooner? Perfect. Just perfect. Now . . . how to get them together?

She pushed the problem to the back of her mind, confident that she'd think of something eventually. A larger problem loomed in her thoughts, prodded by the slight ache in her lower back. Damn, the doctor'd told her to rest every afternoon, but with Thor coming home she'd forgotten.

Uneasily she wondered if Thor was quite prepared for yet another hostage to fortune, this one a scrap of humanity with his own blood flowing through its tiny veins. It was the final, most irrevocable commitment of all, and one they hadn't talked about. Unplanned, of course, and the doctor seemed a bit concerned about Pepper's tiny pelvis, but Pepper herself was deliriously happy with the news.

Knowing her husband, she felt certain that Thor would be, too, once he got over the shock. She decided not to tell him that the doctor had predicted a cesarean delivery after hearing of her large husband. She'd break that to him later. For now . . . Pepper took a deep breath and patted her only slightly rounded stomach.

"There's no going back now, sweetie," she said, and giggled.

She heard the roar of the Corvette then, smiling as all three pets took off for the front door. She turned down the burner under her Irish stew—authentic, Jean would say—and waited in the kitchen to meet her husband.

Thor came in a few moments later, casual in jeans and a sweater. Tut was riding in his accustomed manner on one shoulder, Brutus was tucked beneath an arm, and Fifi frisked happily at his side. The cat was nattering in his loud Siamese voice, Brutus yapping excitedly, and Fifi whining.

Laughing gray eyes met hers from the doorway. "One man's family," Thor said wryly.

"Is it my turn yet?" Pepper asked meekly.

"Are you kidding?" He set the cat and dog on the floor, patted Fifi with an automatically soothing murmur, and reached for his wife.

Emerging from the embrace with very little breath to spare for speech, Pepper managed to say happily, "I just love homecomings!"

"Mmm. Me too." Thor nuzzled her neck, breathing in the soft scent that was peculiarly hers. "You look very fetching today, beloved. I don't often see you in a skirt."

"I thought it'd be a nice change," she murmured, not telling him that only the realization that all her jeans were too tight had sent her scurrying to a doctor.

"Very nice." When the oven timer went off, he released her with an obvious reluctance that delighted her. He sat down on a stool at the breakfast bar, watching her remove a pie from the oven.

"That smells good. So does whatever you've got in that pot."

"Irish stew."

"I'll gain ten pounds."

"If you haven't by now, you never will." Pepper turned off the oven. "Was it a rough one? It took less time than usual." They'd learned to talk about Thor's work, however briefly. It helped Pepper to know exactly what was involved in his work, and it seemed to help Thor as well.

"No, it was fairly simple. There was some high wind, but once it died down, we didn't have any trouble."

"Good."

Abruptly Thor asked, "Have you seen Cody lately?"

Pepper set the pie aside to cool and looked at him in surprise. "Yesterday as a matter of fact. I ran into him in Bangor and we had lunch. Why?"

Thor grinned slightly. "If I were a jealous man . . ."

"You know better than that."

"Thankfully yes, I do. Nevertheless, we'll have to do something about Cody. I'd think your matchmaking instincts would be revolted by his continued bachelorhood."

"They are, and I'm working on it."

Looking interested, Thor asked simply, "Who?"

"Her name's Brooke Kennedy, and you don't know her; I'll tell you about her later. Why'd you ask about Cody?"

Thor frowned. "Well, he left a package for me at the airport; I thought you might know something about it."

"What kind of package?"

Wordlessly Thor rose and left the kitchen, returning a moment later with the package. It was a white box tied with a bright red ribbon. He slid the ribbon off, removed the top, and propped the package up on the bar, revealing the contents.

Looking out of the box with bright button eyes was an average, ordinary, run-of-the-mill Teddy bear. Around its neck were two ribbons tied in bows, one blue and one pink.

Pepper stared at it, knowing that her mouth was open. Damn the man! How'd he guessed? She hadn't told him a thing! Then Pepper realized that she must have been dreamy-eyed and vague after hearing the doctor's news. Trust Cody to put two and two together, she thought wryly.

Thor was sitting on the stool again, gazing at the package with a frown. "I know Cody likes to add to the menagerie apparently, but why a stuffed bear, for God's sake?"

Turning off the burner under the stew, Pepper crossed to stand between Thor's knees, linking her arms around his neck with a smile. "Cody was just trying to steal my thunder, darling, and I'll strangle him the next time I see him."

"Steal your thunder?" Thor slid his arms around her, drawing her close. "What're you talking about?"

"Well, he couldn't have known for sure, since I didn't say a word to him, but he must have guessed. And you say I have a poker face!"

"Pepper."

"Well, I didn't want to tell you like this, dammit. I'd planned a cozy dinner with candlelight and wine and soft music—"

"Pepper . . ." Thor was beginning to look nervous. "Just what are you trying very hard not to come right out and say?"

"I'm pregnant," she said baldly.

"You're . . . ?" Thor's nervous expression acquired a dazed tilt. "You're . . ."

"Pregnant." She spelled it. "And I hope you don't mind, darling, because I kind of like the idea. I mean, what's one more hostage? That front bedroom will make a marvelous nursery, don't you think?"

"Nursery," he murmured blankly. Bemused gray eyes stared into hers for a moment, then cleared suddenly. "Are you all right?" he demanded worriedly. "Why've you been cooking? Where's Jean? She should be doing this!"

"Jean's at her sister's house; the poor woman fell and broke her leg a couple of days ago, and Jean's helping out. And I'm fine, darling. You really don't mind about the baby?"

"Mind? I—" Thor cleared his throat strongly. "No, I don't— It's just that I've never thought about being a father."

"You have about six months to get used to the idea."

"Six months?" He swallowed. "That's not very much time."

"You won't need very much time." Pepper smiled at him lovingly. "Daddy's little man or Daddy's little princess—either way, you'll be a wonderful father, darling."

Thor hugged her suddenly, burying his face in the curve of her neck. "Damn you and your chasing," he said thickly. "Just look what you've gotten me into!"

"I think it's the other way around!"

He lifted his head, eyes suspiciously bright, and

smiled at her. "I love you, you know. More and more every day. And I can't wait to meet Daddy's little whatever."

"Daddy's little hostage." Pepper kissed him tenderly. "I love you, Thor. I'll always love you."

Suddenly teasing, Thor murmured, "Even if I warn Cody you're after his scalp?"

"Even if you warn Cody. You know I play fair, darling. I'll warn him myself."

Thor lifted an eyebrow. "That sure of yourself? Just who is this Brooke Kennedy, anyway?"

Pepper told him, at length and in great detail, and her husband was looking a bit startled by the end of the recitation.

"She doesn't sound like Cody's type at all."

"She's perfect for him."

"The matchmaker's final word, eh?"

"I got you, didn't I?"

"You certainly did. Poor Cody."

"Save your sympathy. Cody'll be too busy to feel sorry for himself."

"Too busy?"

"Chasing Brooke."

"Oh, she'll run, will she?"

"In a wonderfully confusing circle. It ought to be interesting."

"Uh. Beloved?"

"Yes, darling?"

"You're dangerous."

"However—?"

"However, I have this curious love of danger. . . ."

THE EDITOR'S CORNER

With the Olympic Games in Los Angeles much on our minds these past days, we remembered a letter we got last year from Barbara York of Houston, Texas. Barbara gave us a compliment that was truly heartwarming. "If there were an Olympics for category romances," she wrote, "LOVESWEPT would win all the gold medals!"

I don't know about winning them *all* (we're always impressed by the works of talented writers in our competitors' lines). I do know, though, that all our LOVESWEPT authors and staff strive constantly for excellence in our romance publishing program . . . and that we love our work!

And now to the "solid gold" LOVESWEPTS you can expect from us next month.

Joan J. Domning is back with a marvelously evocative romance, **LAHTI'S APPLE,** LOVESWEPT #63. How this romance appeals to the senses. Place, time, sight, sound, tender emotion leap from the pages in this sensitive, yet passionate story of the growing love between heroine Laurian Bryant and hero Keska Lahti. A disillusioned musician, Keska has started an apple orchard and Laurian moves into his world to bring him fully alive. The fragrance of an apple orchard through its seasons . . . the poignant, sometimes melancholy strains of violin and cello are delightfully interwoven with delicate strands of tension between two unforgettable lovers. **LAHTI'S APPLE** stays with you, haunts like a lovely melody.

And what a treat is in store for you in Joan Bramsch's second romance, **A KISS TO MAKE IT BETTER,** LOVESWEPT #64. There's playfulness, joy, humor in

(continued)

this charming love story of Jenny Larsen, a former nurse, and Dr. Jon McCallem. But there is another dimension to this romance—the healing power of love for two sensitive human beings hurt by life's inequities. A simply beautiful story!

Billie Green appeared at one of our teas for LOVE-SWEPT readers not long ago. A lady in the audience got up during the question and answer period with authors and said, "Billie, I love your autobiographical sketches in your books almost as much as I love the books themselves. All I've got to say is thank God for your mother!" There was a big, spontaneous round of applause. Well, that "tetched" quality Billie credits her mother with having passed on to her is present with all its whimsical and enriching power in **THE LAST HERO,** LOVESWEPT #65. Billie's heroine, Toby Baxter, is funny . . . but she's also so fragile a personality that you'll find yourself moist of eye and holding your breath. Then Jake Hammond, a dream of a hero—tender, powerful, yet with supreme control— begins to take gentle charge of Toby's life . . . to exorcise her demons. Different, dramatic, **THE LAST HERO** is a remarkable love story.

IN A CLASS BY ITSELF, LOVESWEPT #66, by Sandra Brown is aptly titled. It *is* an absolutely spellbinding, one-of-a-kind love story. Dani Quinn is one of Sandra's most lovable heroines ever. And Logan Webster has got to be the most devastatingly attractive man Sandra's ever dreamed up. That walk, that walk, that fabulous walk of Logan's. I guarantee you'll never forget it—nor any of the other elements in this breathtakingly emotional, totally sensual romance. In my judgment, **IN A CLASS BY ITSELF** is Sandra Brown's most delicious, heartwarming love story—in short, my favorite of all her books. You won't want to miss it!

You know, these four LOVESWEPTS *do* have the properties of real gold—shine and brilliance on the surface, the true and "forever" value beneath.

Hope you agree.

Warm regards,

Carolyn Nichols

Carolyn Nichols
  Editor
LOVESWEPT
Bantam Books, Inc.
666 Fifth Avenue
New York, NY 10103